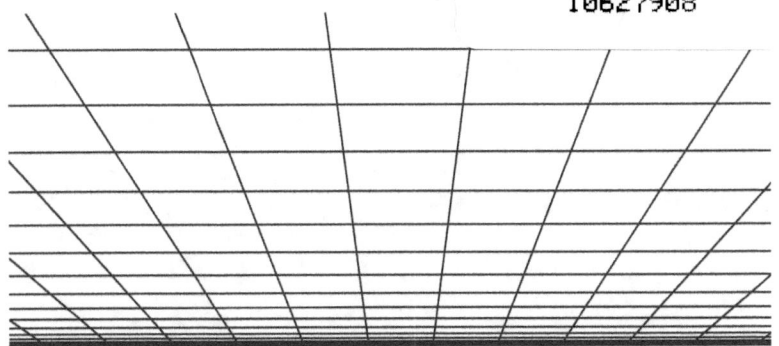

REVIVING DADE
PROJECT DEEP
BOOK THREE

BECCA JAMESON

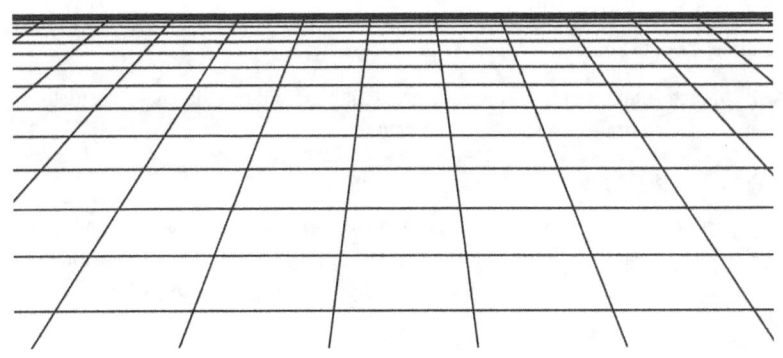

ACKNOWLEDGMENTS

I really have to thank everyone who listened to me ramble on and on about this series for months while I worked out the plot and figured out where we were going. It's a totally new genre for me. (Well, I mean except for the fact that it's still erotic romance! Let's not get carried away.) So, it took a lot of planning.

The concept came to me in the early hours of the morning in a dream when I wasn't quite awake yet. (Okay, gotta pause again here to say that "early" is a relative term. I don't do "early." Nothing in my world is actually "early." I just mean whatever time the last hour of my sleep occurred. Probably more like ten in the morning.)

In my dream, there were these scientists in a government bunker. They were studying diseases. They got sick. They had to be cryonically preserved... And from there, a series was launched. I spent a great deal of time studying cryonics and learning the difference between cryonics, cryobiology, and cryogenics--which are very different things.

I worked very hard to ensure that my terminology was correct with respect to the field of cryonics, though I obviously took a great deal of artistic liberty when reviving the preserved since alas, as far as we know, no one has been reanimated to this date.

Many thanks to Christa Soule for plotting with me when we were in the early stages, and then when we were in the middle stages, and still to this day.

Thanks to my husband and countless friends who listened to me and added their two cents.

CHAPTER 1

"The Notebook? Are you serious?" Blair stared at Emily hard, forcing herself not to roll her eyes. Chick flicks were not her thing, especially not sappy ones. But Emily was the one who'd missed out on over ten years' worth of movies, so Blair wasn't about to say a word. If her friend wanted to spend the evening crying over Nicholas Sparks, Blair would endure it.

Emily giggled as she opened the fridge. "Hey, I read the book, but I never got to see the movie."

"I'm pretty sure it's older than ten years," Blair pointed out, as she took a beer from Emily's hand and shoved her hip off the counter.

"Do you think I had a lot of free time in the few years before I was preserved?" Emily asked.

She had a point. Before she'd been cryonically preserved for the past ten years, she had spent several years buried in this bunker working for the government on Project DEEP (Disease & Epidemic Eradication & Prevention). The final disease she had been studying, frantically working toward a cure, had also been the one to land her, twenty other team members, and General Winston Custodio in cryostats. Thanks to a freak lab accident,

AP12, a fatal viral form of anemia, infected everyone in the medical wing.

"Considering the work ethic you've demonstrated since I met you, I'm going to say probably not," Blair replied. Emily worked night and day.

So did her boyfriend, Ryan Anand, who was currently sitting at the kitchen table on the other side of the room with his head buried in his computer and his brow furrowed. Both of them were as dedicated to their work as any human Blair had ever met.

In fact, it must be an affliction all these medical researchers suffered from because both of Ryan's parents had been reanimated in the last few months too, and they were equally dedicated workhorses.

Emily held a soda in her hand as she plopped down on the couch. "I'm not sure you're actually allowed to drink beer while you watch Nicholas Sparks, but I'll let it slide," she joked.

"I'm not sure you're allowed to watch anything while sitting this close to the television," Blair returned, also teasing. Ryan and Emily lived inside the bunker in one of the new suites that were built a few years ago to house the full-time employees. The living room area was incredibly tight.

"Fuck," Ryan suddenly shouted. He followed that by launching his pen at the wall and then shoving his chair back. Hand threaded in his hair, he turned toward them. His face was red.

Emily jumped up from the couch, set her soda on the coffee table, and faced Ryan. "What happened?"

Blair's teeth were on edge. She'd known Ryan for a long time, and she'd never seen him lose his cool. Not once. Something he was working on had seriously pissed him off.

His chest rose and fell with every breath.

"Ryan?" Emily said, her voice lower. She had known Ryan for six months, ever since she had been the first person to be reanimated from the original Project DEEP team.

He released his hair to run a hand down his face. "We have a problem."

"What is it?" Emily asked.

Blair felt out of place, as if she shouldn't be here. But it couldn't be helped. She would feel even more awkward about easing out of the suite.

"We can't give Dade the cure." His shoulders fell as he spoke.

Dade Menke was scheduled to come out of his coma the next day. After four weeks in the reanimation chamber, each patient then spent four weeks in an induced coma to allow their organs to fully rejuvenate before they were awakened.

Blair knew a great deal of the details. Assigned to security detail at this bunker for the last seven years, she was as informed as possible about what the team of medical researchers did at the facility.

Emily eased across the room and set a hand on Ryan's arm. "Why not?"

"He's got the genetic marker for aplastic anemia 2. I can't believe I didn't see this in his charts before now."

"Oh, no. Ryan, I'm so sorry."

Blair couldn't keep herself from asking questions. She had no idea what they were talking about, but it had to be bad. "What does that mean?"

Emily turned around. "Aplastic anemia is when the bone marrow stops producing enough blood cells. Unfortunately there have been several instances in the last year when patients were given the treatment for AP12 only to have it jumpstart latent aplastic anemia they didn't even know they carried. AA2 is a mutation of the common form."

"So you can't give him the cure for AP12 because it will kill him?"

"Basically," Ryan stated. "Dammit. The guy is thirty-five years old. He's just spent ten years suspended in time. I can't believe when he wakes up tomorrow, I have to tell him he's still going to die."

Emily wiped her eyes as she headed across the room to grab a tissue. She would be the one in the room to take this the hardest. Dade had been her coworker. Blair hadn't been there ten years ago. And Ryan, who had dedicated his entire life to finding a cure and putting together a new team to reanimate the first team, was only twenty when everyone was preserved.

"Project DEEP has been working on a cure for AA2 for months now. Maybe..." Emily's voice wavered.

Blair could only surmise that most likely Emily was grasping at straws. Blair knew next to nothing about medical research, but she was smart enough to realize it took years to find a cure for any disease. Dade wouldn't have that kind of time.

Even though she had never met the guy and she hadn't even seen pictures of him, her heart seized to hear his age. She too was thirty-five. She couldn't imagine someone coming to her tomorrow to tell her they had the cure for her first fatal disease but injecting it would give her another equally fatal disease.

Emily's voice was soft when she asked her next question. "How much time do you think he might have if you don't give him the AP12 cure and instead work against the symptoms?"

"I don't know. We've proven that the total blood replacement he received a month ago will buy him time. It worked for you. But in your case, we only waited three weeks. There's no way to know when you would have developed AP12 symptoms. And when we reanimated my parents, we gave them the treatment immediately." He pulled his chair back to the table and pushed it in.

Blair hated seeing him this defeated. Emily too. What a blow to their research.

Ryan closed his computer and picked it up. "I'm going to go work in the lab. You two enjoy your movie." He kissed Emily on the cheek and left the suite.

There was no way in the world they could sit and watch a sad movie after that revelation, but Blair took her seat anyway. Emily would need a friend.

The two of them had met only five months ago when Blair was assigned to Emily's protection for one day, but they had bonded and formed a friendship that would last a lifetime.

After a few minutes of silence, Emily sat up straighter. "The media will have a field day with this. Shit. Plus, the rest of the reanimations could be compromised if he dies. The government might force us to slow down to be certain every member will survive." She slapped her forehead with her palm.

Blair cringed. "Can we keep the media from finding out, at least?"

Emily chuckled wryly. "Sure. Like we kept them from finding out about me and then Tushar and Trish. How long did that last? All of twenty-four hours? The vultures are just waiting for a mistake."

CHAPTER 2

Two weeks later...

Dade's head was pounding as he held the data in front of him with shaky hands.

"I've gone over it a dozen times. I've also redone your bloodwork several times. I might not have even noticed the mutated genes if I hadn't seen the same thing in every patient who didn't survive the treatment for AP12." Ryan's voice trailed off.

Dade lifted his gaze to meet Emily's where she stood on his other side, one hand on his shoulder. He'd never seen a single living being look quite that sorrowful. Of course, he also hadn't looked in a mirror yet.

After dropping the papers on his lap, he leaned his head back and closed his eyes. He'd been up walking enough times to get his ass out of this hospital bed and get stronger, but suddenly he didn't have the will anymore.

Something had felt *off* from the moment Dade awoke two weeks ago. Ryan Anand had been his primary daily visitor, and although he spoke often of the project and updated Dade on its progress, he had also held something back.

Dade had felt the omission in the air every day. People failed to make eye contact with him. They glanced away. Their lips were pursed. Sometimes they looked too sad or didn't say enough.

He'd been too chicken to ask for specifics yet. All his concentration had been focused on getting his ass out of the hospital bed as his strength increased in small increments. Apparently, he was right on target with the first three people to be reanimated. It took time. At least that's what he'd been told.

Now he knew why the air got sucked out of the room every time someone visited.

Dade still couldn't wrap his mind around the fact that the person in charge of this new team was Tushar and Trish's son. The kid he'd met only a few times a decade ago was now a medical professional only five years younger than himself.

Emily looked the same. He couldn't wait to get reacquainted with Tushar and Trish if they ever returned from some ranch in Montana where they were hiding from the piranhas.

With each breath, his chest rose and fell, lifting the papers on his torso. Not giving a single fuck what anyone thought, he flicked the data onto the floor.

Emily and Ryan at least had the grace not to flinch or comment.

"I'm so sorry," Ryan finally said. "I'm working around the clock to come up with a way..."

Emily sounded like she was going to cry every time she spoke, and he didn't remember her being emotional a decade ago. Ten years—that seemed like last week. "Let's not lose hope, okay? We don't know how long the blood replacement will buy you. Maybe it will be much longer than we imagine."

"Lose hope?" Dade asked sarcastically. "Sure. Okay. I just spent ten years in hibernation like a bear only to wake up and learn that it was all for nothing."

A tear ran down Emily's face, and he felt bad for being an ass, but he needed to remind himself this wasn't about her.

He rubbed his temples and closed his eyes again. He was full of shit. He'd done very little *but* sleep so far since awakening two weeks ago. The first week, he'd needed it badly. The second week, he was using the excuse to hide. Hide from himself and everyone else.

This damn bunker used to be his home. It was his life blood. Now, it felt like a death chamber. He knew from multiple conversations with General Temple Levenson—the same woman who had been in charge of the project ten years ago—that the situation out in the real world was not pleasant.

Apparently religious zealots and the media were camped out at the gate in large numbers, hoping to catch a glimpse of the freaks who were being reanimated inside. Even though Dade had yet to see the show, their presence made him nervous.

Ryan sighed. "I don't mean to sound overly optimistic, but we have some options."

Dade blew out a breath, not bothering to open his eyes. "Watcha got up your sleeve, Dr. Anand?" He knew he sounded snarky, but he didn't give a fuck.

"I'm working on an experimental drug. Given enough time, it might work."

"Tested?" Dade asked. He already knew the answer.

"Not on humans, no." Ryan's voice was low. "But I think we can buy you some time while I keep working. I don't want you to give up. Several drugs were developed to slow down the progress of AP12 while we were working on the cure. They have been extremely effective.

"Plus, you have the added bonus of not having any symptoms right now because your blood was replaced. It will take a while for your bone marrow to start attacking the new blood. Blood transfusions combined with some of these medications will help."

Dade finally lifted his face and met Ryan's gaze. He knew his next words were going to drip with sarcasm. "So you're talking months instead of weeks? Swell. Let me get on my bucket list right now. It's short, really. I've always pictured myself growing old in a nice mountain cabin with nothing but the sounds of nature to keep me company. How long do I have before the quality of my life is not worth it?"

Ryan swallowed. He didn't know. Nobody knew.

Dade scooted farther down the bed and closed his eyes again. "I think I'll take a nap. Thanks for the pep talk."

The next time Dade opened his eyes, he startled for a moment. He did that often. Ever since coming out of the coma, he found himself jolting awake as if there had been a loud noise or he'd had a nightmare. Except there never seemed to be evidence of any noises, and he couldn't remember his dreams.

He was thirsty, but he didn't have the energy or the will to bother reaching for the pitcher of water at his side, so he simply stared at the ceiling—his new habit.

He'd already been through a death. It had been devastating. It had taken its toll on him mentally. Not a near-death experience. He had died. For all intents and purposes, he had died. He'd known for months that he had been infected with a fatal virus that would kill him.

It didn't matter that he had been aware there was a remote possibility in the future he could be revived. *Remote* was the key word. His team of twenty-one had worked on the cure for AP12 for over five years, ever since General Winston Custodio had come to the bunker infected with the virus. He hadn't survived. He was the first person they had cryonically preserved.

After years of research, a broken beaker had caused the virus to become airborne and infect the entire team. Over the next few months, one by one, each of them had fallen ill. All of them had agreed to be preserved one floor below in this very bunker.

All of them had also agreed to be preserved before they died naturally.

They were scientists. They understood the likelihood of ever being revived would be slim if they waited for their bodies to completely fail. So, technically, yes, they had been legally dead at the time of preservation, but human intervention had been the cause.

The possibility that Dade might one day be revived had been too unlikely for him to put any real stock in it. He'd never truly trusted it.

Dade Menke had died.

So, fuck the weird deity with a strange sense of humor who thought it might be fun to toy with him by reviving him only to kill him again.

How was this happening? He had hoped if he went to sleep and woke up again he would find out it had all been a dream, but no such luck. He was still lying in this bed. He was still infected with two forms of anemia. He was still going to die.

As that realization settled over him for the second time that day, he squeezed his eyes shut. He'd already been through the process of accepting death once before. Only a cruel God would make him do this again. After two weeks of thinking he was going to get a new chance at life, he couldn't believe how the path had taken this twist.

What had he done in life to deserve this fate? He was a good person. He'd dedicated his life to saving others. Surely the universe could see fit to give him another chance. *Please, God.*

Deep breaths. Pleading with God wasn't going to help. He needed to swallow this pill and accept that he was going to die. Again. In this fucking bunker. He didn't have much time. It would be spent in this damn room on this damn bed with Ryan and his team running around trying to slow time.

Why bother to join the let's-have-hope bandwagon? How useless. He was weak and tired. It would be easier to accept his fate and let go of any plans he might have had to get out of this bunker and live a valuable life.

He let out a long slow breath.

"It's not a bad idea, you know."

Dade nearly jumped out of bed at the sound of the female voice coming from behind him. He lifted his head, heart pumping, and twisted to find a woman he'd never met sitting in an armchair in the corner.

No. She wasn't just sitting. She was lounging. Casually. She was literally comfortably propped in the stupid vinyl olive-green armchair. Sideways. Her head leaning back against one palm, her feet dangling over the other arm. Totally incongruent was the fact that she wore a uniform. Navy pants. Medium blue shirt. She had to be one of the security detail.

He continued to stare at her, unable to form words. Her blond hair was pulled into a bun, so he had no idea how long it might be. She also wore minimal makeup. She didn't need it.

What stood out was her eyes—piercing blue. They seemed to glow from across the room.

"What are you talking about? Who are you?" he finally managed to sputter, his mouth so dry the words came out scratchy.

She swung her legs around, set her hands on her knees, and pushed to standing. Silently, she came across the room and picked up the pitcher of water on the small table at his side. She poured him a glass and then had the audacity to grab the remote at his side and adjust the mattress so that he was forced to sit up straighter.

He watched her, mesmerized. Part of him assumed he was still asleep, imagining her, finally having a dream. He wanted to swat the cup of water out of her hand and tell her to leave him the fuck alone, but he couldn't find the will.

11

When she apparently had him in the position she preferred, she picked up his hand and wrapped his fingers around the cup as if he were a damn invalid who couldn't have done so by himself.

He didn't bring the water to his lips, but at least he didn't throw it in her face either. That took will.

Damn bossy woman. She hadn't spoken another word yet, and already he could tell she was used to getting her way.

"I thought you were going to sleep all day," she finally said. She met his gaze, those damn blue eyes piercing him, and continued. "I'm Blair Rollans."

He lifted a brow. "So?"

She smiled condescendingly. "I've been assigned as your bodyguard."

"My what?" His voice rose as he leaned forward, forgetting the cup which tipped too far. Water spilled over the side of his hand.

Blair gently reached out and righted his hand, her smaller one wrapped around his fingers, remaining a few seconds as if to confirm that he was aware and had the damn cup under control.

"What are you? Personal security detail? What the hell do I need a bodyguard for? Did the bunker start letting anyone who wants to wander onto the grounds and stroll down the hallways?"

She smiled again, this time broader. Devastating. If she graced whoever her significant other was with that smile often, the guy was surely putty in her hands. "We're not going to be staying in the bunker."

He lifted a brow again. Why did it seem like she had way more information about him than he did?

Suddenly he remembered her opening line. *It's not a bad idea, you know.* "Please tell me this doesn't have anything to do with my snide comment about a bucket list."

Another earth-moving grin. "He remembers." She patted his hand. "Drink your water. It might make you sound less growly. We leave tomorrow morning."

CHAPTER 3

"This is a joke, right?" Dade watched as Blair leaned against the doorframe of his room, casually. She wasn't wearing a uniform this time. In fact, he might not have recognized her at all if it hadn't been for her deep blue eyes. She had on jeans that rode low on her hips, a cream-colored thermal shirt, and hiking boots. Her blond hair was in a long thick braid that fell over one shoulder. Her stature was slight compared to his. He put her at about five foot five. But he could also sense she was not a woman to be messed with.

She was definitely not a girly girl, but she couldn't hide how attractive she was either. He imagined her with four brothers fighting to fit in with them as a child while insisting she could do anything they could do better.

He had to shake the absurd thought from his head. Why the hell did he care if she had siblings or not? He had no business even being curious.

She glanced at her watch. "Nope. If you want to take a shower before we leave, you should probably hurry. We're leaving in fifteen minutes."

Emily slid into the room around Blair, her face beaming.

"Hey." She switched to a frown. "Why are you still in that bed?" She snapped her fingers. "Get up. Get dressed."

Ryan had already scolded him about an hour ago about getting out of bed. He didn't need two women doing the same thing. "This plan is ludicrous. I'm not going to some mountain cabin to die."

Blair lifted a finger. "This much is true. You're going there to *live*."

Dade crossed his arms and glared at the two women. "I'm bigger than the two of you put together." He sounded absurd. After ten years in preservation and two weeks of inactive defiance, there wasn't a snowball's chance in hell he could so much as stand without swaying. He wouldn't be able to fight a forty-pound five-year-old.

Emily giggled. "You're weaker, though. I've been working out since my revival. And Blair works out more than anyone I know. She takes her job seriously. You're going to have to hustle to keep up with her."

He growled. "This is not happening."

"So you intend to lie in that bed for the rest of your life, wallowing in self-pity?" Emily asked.

"Yep."

She set her hands on her hips. "The Dade I knew was energetic, funny, and full of piss and vinegar. Even in the most stressful times, he managed to pull a prank or make a joke to break up the monotony so we could all be more productive in the lab."

"Yeah, well, that guy died." *Apparently he's also slated to die again.*

Ignoring him, Emily continued. "So, by my guess, you won't notice any of the symptoms from AP12 for weeks or months. I waited three weeks before getting treatment, and I hadn't exhibited a single symptom yet. Not even in my bloodwork."

"What's your point?" He had no intention of finding the good in this situation. He was too tired to bother.

As if there weren't enough women in the room, his boss, Temple, made an appearance. "Hey, I hear you're going on a little vacation."

Three fucking women now stared at him with forced smiles.

He scowled. "A vacation. Is that what we're calling it?"

Temple nodded. "Yes. And I'll have you know my cabin is amazing. It's not some dusty, dank rickety shack in the woods. It's a vacation property. I've been renting it out for years. I've never had a bad review."

"The cabin is yours?" No one had mentioned that detail.

"Yep. Three bedrooms. Two baths. Fireplace. Modern appliances. It's so far off the beaten path that it's difficult to find. No one will ever know you're there. The security system is top of the line. You'll be safe." She turned to face Blair. "Plus I can assure you Blair is one of the best. I'd trust her with my life."

Emily agreed. "It's true. I *have* trusted her with my life."

Blair rolled her eyes. "I hardly think you're a stellar example of my abilities at protection. I won't be using you on my resume anytime soon. Did you forget the part where I got shot and you got kidnapped?"

"Wait? What?" Dade sat up straighter. "You got shot?" He shifted his gaze to Emily. "You got kidnapped?"

Emily nodded. "I did indeed. Have you not caught on to the fact that there are a lot of people out there who don't approve of our existence?"

He had been told that. He simply didn't care. It was never going to matter to him.

Temple came farther into the room. "Lucky for you, news of your reanimation hasn't leaked. I'd like to keep it that way."

Dade curled his hands into fists at his sides. "Has it escaped everyone's notice that I'll probably be dead before any news about me could possibly leak?"

"Not possible." The latest person to enter the room was Ryan. *Great.*

"You can't even give me a timeframe," Dade pointed out. "It's not as if I could stroll out the front gate and wander through society. I would infect half the population and start an epidemic."

He'd read some of the updated information Ryan had provided him, but not enough. He was pretty sure he remembered reading that few people had been infected in North America, and all of those who were infected had recently traveled abroad.

A vaccine had been developed, but it hadn't been widely dispersed yet since it hadn't been necessary in the States with so few cases and a perfectly effective cure.

Naturally, everyone who worked in the bunker or on the grounds had received the immunization.

"You're absolutely right," Temple agreed. "That's why we're going to sneak you off the grounds in the back of a delivery truck that will take you and Rollans to a specified location where you'll switch to a car and take it to the cabin."

"You have this all planned out so well. Why exactly didn't anyone bother to check with me before you plotted out how my dying days would be spent?" He didn't give a single solid fuck that he was being an asshole. Nor did he care that any psychologist would point out that feeling sorry for himself was not the best use of his remaining time.

"It's more than that," Temple said. "The struggle to keep your team alive is real. After what happened yesterday, I need you to do this for the team."

Ryan groaned.

Dade narrowed his gaze. "What happened yesterday?"

Temple's shoulders fell. "Sorry. I thought you knew."

Dade stared at everyone in the room with wide eyes. "Apparently not."

Ryan took a deep breath. "My parents were found and attacked where they were hiding on a ranch in Montana."

"What the fuck? Ryan? Why didn't you tell me? Are they okay?" Dade could feel the heat rising on his face. This was serious. Emily had been kidnapped, and Tushar and Trish had been attacked? Holy fuck.

"They're fine. They escaped. They're heading this way tomorrow."

Dade blew out a breath of relief. He rubbed the back of his neck with one hand while trying to piece this story together. "Why on earth would you want me to leave the bunker if it's so damn unsafe out there?" He shuddered. Tushar and Trish had been the anchors of his team. They had not only been the oldest members, but also the first to join the team. Everyone had answered to them. Everyone adored them.

Ryan glanced out into the hallway and then shut the door. He stepped farther into the room, rubbing his hands together. "The truth is, we have a mole."

"Pardon?" This saga kept getting worse.

Ryan nodded. "Not a single living soul outside of this room is going to know where you went or even that you left this bunker. We can't take the risk that someone will find you."

Dade smirked. "Unless one of you is the mole," he joked.

No one laughed. Apparently they took this seriously.

"I was joking. Geez." He glanced around at everyone in the room. Ryan had spent his life ensuring the team could be reanimated. Emily had been on the first team herself. Temple was the general who had been in charge of the bunker from day one. That only left Blair.

Dade didn't know Blair, but he had to assume the rest of the people in the room trusted her enough to put her in charge of his safety. Besides, she had been shot protecting Emily. That wouldn't lead anyone to think she was playing for the enemy.

"We take everyone's life seriously around here," Temple added. "Look, I'll be blunt. I don't like you cooped up in this bunker, moping around. It's not fair to you..."

"And it's not good for morale inside the bunker. I get it." He sighed. Of course. It would be hard on everyone who already worked long shifts seven days a week to have to skirt around a dying man with a surly disposition.

"That's not what I meant," Temple defended.

"Yeah. It is. How hard would it be for someone to find me if I'm going to your personal cabin?"

"You aren't. I don't own a cabin."

He gave his head a quick shake. "What? I'm starting to think I've suffered brain damage."

Temple smiled. "You haven't. We all just created that story so that it would spread around. If anyone starts digging, they'll find nothing and waste their time trying."

He lifted his brows. "You've thought of everything."

"Yep." Emily's infectious smile thawed him a little. She even stepped right up beside him and took his hand. "I want you to go. Enjoy life. Breathe. The entire team will be here working hard to find a way to cure you. Have faith in us. I don't want you to wander around here half aware of our daily accomplishments. It would be too stressful for you."

Dade glanced past her to find Blair watching him closely. "Even if I did agree to your plan and the elaborate reasons you've all presented, I wouldn't want a soul to have to spend their days trapped with me in some remote location watching me die. Do you all dislike Blair so much that you want her out of your hair?" He couldn't help but shoot her a half smile.

She cocked her head to one side. "You are not going to die. Not on my watch. I'm a trained bodyguard, Dade. It's my job to guard whoever I'm assigned to. I take that job very seriously. Nothing will happen to you in my care."

He stared at her. How many people had she protected? She could have been military. She had that vibe. He wondered if she'd been in combat situations, perhaps even overseas. He didn't even know what wars the country was currently fighting or might have engaged in over the past decade.

"Blair, I'm going to die," he pointed out.

She shrugged. "We're all going to die. But you're not doing anything of the sort in the near future. I forbid it."

At that, he actually laughed. For the first time since Ryan had told him about his condition yesterday morning, he found something funny. "Are you always this bossy?"

"Only when I'm awake." She shoved off the wall where she'd stood this entire time and clapped her hands together. "We have to get going."

He didn't respond as she turned around, opened the door, and left the room. A sense of loss climbed up his spine at her exit. Her energy had filled the space, and she took it with her, leaving the room with less oxygen.

Less life.

"One more thing," Ryan said, as soon as Blair was gone.

"There's more?" Dade took a breath and glanced around the room. Whatever it was, the rest of the occupants knew about it.

Ryan lifted Dade's wrist and pointed to a spot where his IV had been until recently. "There's a small tracking device in your arm just under the skin. You would never notice it if I didn't tell you."

Dade stiffened. "Why?"

Emily grabbed his other hand. "We all have one. Just in case."

"Only a few people are aware we put them in you," Ryan added. "I'm sure you'll forget about it, and no one will ever need to use it, but it's there for your safety."

Dade shifted his attention to Emily again. "That's how they found you."

She nodded, pursing her lips.

Dade ran a hand through his hair. "Okay, duly noted. Tracker in my arm. I'm like a secret spy."

Ryan continued. "It's not without problems. I mean, yes, we were able to use it to find Emily, but the tracker was also used to pinpoint my parents' location."

"Great. So you've embedded a tracker in my arm to save me, but it can also be used by the enemy to hunt me down?"

"Yeah. Basically."

"And who the hell was able to access that information?"

Ryan sighed. "We don't know yet. We don't even know if it's an internal operation or a hacker from outside. Which is why I'm going to deactivate it until we find the mole. I'll only reactivate it in case of an emergency."

Dade shuddered. *There's a damn GPS tracker in me.* Welcome to jumping forward a decade.

CHAPTER 4

As Blair sat in the back of the medical supply vehicle, holding on to the metal bar at the side to keep from falling over, she tried to calm her mind. It was damn cold outside, and the back of the truck was not heated, so her hands were freezing where she gripped the bar. She forced herself to ignore the discomfort.

Blair had no intention of letting Dade see even an inch of her weakness. In fact, she rarely let a living soul see that side of her. So infrequently that she could count on one hand the number of times she'd cried or been consumed with emotion, and most of those times had been alone, so they didn't count.

The most recent time she'd been unable to hide her feelings had been that day two weeks ago when Ryan had discovered that Dade had the genetic marker for AA2. After he'd left the suite to head back to the lab, Blair had stayed behind to comfort Emily.

Blair hadn't even seen a picture of Dade at the time. She knew very little about him. She had no physical description at all. She only knew he was a biomedical scientist who had served in the army in order to pay for his education and then been assigned to work on Project DEEP.

She too had served in the army for ten years, but that would have been after his time. Not to mention her service had looked quite a bit different from his. She had done three tours overseas as personal security detail to many different people. It had been a long time since she'd been tasked with specifically guarding someone's life, but she didn't imagine it would involve even half what she'd seen during her service.

She had been at the bunker longer than anyone on the new team. Five years longer. The job had been far more boring when the staff consisted of only the bare amount needed to maintain the facility. For years, the bunker had operated with a skeleton staff until Ryan Anand had gotten closer to a cure and the government had once again funded the project and hired additional members to work on reanimation. Among them was Dr. Damon Bardsley, a cryonicist.

The bunker had been more like a morbid tomb until Ryan and Damon arrived to get down to the business of reviving the previous team. Within months, the team had grown to twelve members, all eager to get the place back up and running, doing what it was meant to accomplish—saving lives.

Blair took a deep breath and gripped the bar on the side of the van tighter as Ryan went over a bump. When she glanced at Dade, she found him staring at her, brows close together. Studying her. He didn't even look away when she caught him.

"We're almost there," Ryan declared from the front seat. They had been driving for nearly an hour, but only because Ryan was following a circuitous route in order to ensure no one followed him. He was wearing a hat and an official company polo of some sort to keep anyone from giving him a second glance as he drove through the throng of protesters at the gate to the facility.

Not a single soul outside of the five people who had been inside the room that morning knew about this mission. Not even the military personnel. Temple had specifically given the order for the men guarding the entrance to wave the truck through without questioning the man at the wheel.

So far they seemed to have succeeded. Though she wasn't sure Dade had the strength to pretend for much longer that he wasn't too weak for this rough ride, sitting on his butt, holding on to whatever he could to keep from getting thrown around. The truck wasn't meant for passengers, and Dade would need a few weeks to regain his full strength.

Finally, Ryan pulled to a stop. He turned around to face his passengers. "You guys okay? I tried to keep from tossing you around like a salad back there."

"We're fine," Blair answered for both of them. She was fairly certain Dade was anything but fine, but she also knew he was stubborn and would never admit to such a thing. His hands were shaking when he released his grip on the metal bar. He didn't meet her gaze as he shuffled toward the hatch and then jumped down to the ground.

A blast of cold wind hit Blair in the face as she followed Dade. The temperature was dropping. It was supposed to snow later that night. She wanted to get to the cabin before it started falling to make sure they had enough firewood inside. She pulled her coat tighter around her and tugged the zipper up to her chin. Not surprising weather for late February in the mountains of Colorado.

Ryan handed Blair a set of keys and pointed to a nondescript tan Jeep Wrangler. "It's four-wheel drive. You won't have any trouble getting to the cabin. I checked out the route yesterday for you. Roads are cleared. Cell service was good, so don't hesitate to call or text. The internet is working. I also stocked the kitchen with everything on your list." He smiled.

Blair took the keys. "Thanks, Ryan. I appreciate your help. I'm sure we'll be fine."

Ryan turned toward a silent Dade. "We're going to fix this," he promised, even though Blair knew as well as Dade that was a longshot. Nevertheless, she fully intended to remain optimistic and drag Dade out of this place of fear and anger to a calmer state of mind where he would stand a chance at life.

Dade rolled his eyes and headed for the passenger side of the Jeep.

Blair smiled at Ryan, thanked him quietly, and climbed into the driver's seat. At least Dade didn't argue about which one of them would be driving. That might have caused a battle.

She took a deep breath and started the Jeep. She didn't intend to treat him with kid gloves or like he was an invalid. She intended to force him to get healthy and fit and back to the land of the living. Her assignment didn't include those tasks. Her job was to protect him and keep him alive. But she never did anything half-assed, so for as long as she was responsible for the man's life, she fully intended to ensure it also got extended and that he snapped out of this bitter place of anger.

She had no idea why she felt so strongly about helping him. She knew nothing about him except that he was surly and angry. Oh, and tall, dark, and handsome. He was a total cliché. His thick hair was in need of a cut, but she kinda liked it that way. It took the edge off his stern facial features.

She knew from Emily that he had been funny, often joking around with everyone else. The morale booster of the team. It made Blair sad that he'd buried that side of himself.

Emily also indicated she felt a change in personality since being revived, so maybe it was something they would all experience. She had to assume it would be life-altering to wake up one day ten years later and find out you had not died. For some, the grass might be greener. For others, it might appear brown and shriveled. Dade fell in the latter category, although rightfully so.

Blair handed Dade her phone. "You navigate. I'll drive."

He took it from her and flipped it around. "Yeah, you do realize I have no idea what you intend for me to do with this, right?"

Did she hear a slight lift of humor in his voice? A glance at his face told her she must have imagined it because he was glaring at her. "Oh shit. Right. Sorry." She took it back, opened the GPS app, and then handed it to him. "Siri will tell us what to do. You can just follow along and make sure she's right. She makes mistakes."

"Who the fuck is Siri?"

Blair grinned wider. "She's the woman in the phone. You can ask her anything. She knows everything. But do that later. Right now, we need her to get us to the cabin."

"Fuck me." He stared at her cell in his hand, and this time she was fairly certain he cracked a smile. Schooling his face back to his scowl, he said, "I thought the cabin part of this saga was a ruse."

"Nope. The cabin really exists. It just doesn't belong to Temple. It's actually mine. And you're going to love it." Blair backed the Jeep up and pulled onto the road, heading the opposite direction as Ryan.

"You have a cabin? How far away is it?"

"Yep. It's only about fifteen minutes from the bunker. Ryan drove us around in circles to make sure we weren't followed. I bought it about four years ago when I realized there was a good chance I would remain assigned to the bunker for longer than a normal assignment. Thought it would be nice to have some place to get away."

"Won't you be just as easily located as Temple would have been?"

"Nope. I've never told anyone I owned it. Not until yesterday, that is. And I only told Ryan where it was located. Keeping it simple. The less people informed, the less likely we are to be discovered." She kept her hands on the wheel and tried not to grip it too hard while she explained herself.

Dade made her fucking nervous the way she could feel his expression piercing her with that damn scowl.

She continued, intent on pretending he wasn't so irate. "I was standing in the hallway while you spoke with Ryan and Emily about your condition. When you mentioned your bucket list."

"Eavesdropping?" Great. Now he was pissed.

She shot him a glance. "No. I was assigned to guard your room. Don't be a dick. It's not necessary."

He eased back and faced the front. "Why did I need a fucking bodyguard inside the bunker? I still don't understand that part."

She pursed her lips, not wanting to elaborate on that topic.

A few moments later, he groaned as he set his elbow on the window and turned his head to face the mountains. "You weren't there to guard me from other people. You were there to guard me from me. Suicide watch."

He was right. He was also sharper than she anticipated. She needed to remember that.

They rode the rest of the way in silence. It wasn't far, but Blair drove around several winding roads a few times just in case. She never once saw another vehicle.

When she finally pulled onto the hidden dirt road that led to the cabin, she released a long breath. She loved this hideaway. She loved that it was peaceful and all hers. Until yesterday when Ryan came up to stock the kitchen and check on things, no one had ever been there. This was the first time she would have a guest.

"You weren't kidding about it being hidden," Dade commented. "I don't even know how you saw the turnoff."

"I've been here hundreds of times. I know it by heart. I was impressed that Ryan found it yesterday from my directions. Though I am pretty thorough. I know every turn to the exact tenth of a mile." She wound her way up the curvy drive until finally pulling to a stop.

Dade tipped his face down a bit to catch a better view of the front. He was so tall that his head was too close to the roof to see well. She watched him as he took in her cabin for the first time.

He wasn't just tall. He was huge. She imagined he'd been extremely fit and worked out a lot before being vitrified—a term she had learned in recent years meant *frozen* but without the water crystals that would damage organs. It was amazing how well each of their bodies endured the ten years of preservation. With a little exercise, Dade would be physically back to his usual self in no time.

"Why doesn't anyone else know about this place? Surely you have at least brought friends up here. Or a man. What about a boyfriend? Husband?" He glanced at her.

She shook her head. "I bought it for the solitude. I don't like to share it. Ryan was the first person to see it since I've owned it."

He stared at her. "You're a loner."

She shrugged. "Not always. But I like to get away. Some military personnel who work at the bunker have places in town. It isn't mandatory. We have housing scattered around the grounds inside the fence of the facility, but I like to be able to leave for a few days and have a place to go when I'm off."

He nodded and opened his door, unfolding his huge frame to climb out of the Jeep. "Is this your Jeep?"

"No. I left my car at the bunker in case anyone might recognize it."

He sauntered toward the front.

For some reason she felt nervous about his first impression. There was no reason to care what he thought of her place, but she did. He was going to live here for the near future. She wanted him to enjoy it. "Does it meet the standards of your first bucket list item?"

He stopped walking, hands tucked in his coat pockets, his breath coming out in puffs of clouds, his head tipped back to take in the entire cabin. "Haven't seen the inside yet," he murmured.

She pursed her lips in frustration, but relaxed when he turned around and shot her one of his half smiles. A devastating look that would melt most women on the spot. She'd seen it a few times now.

"Kidding. It's amazing." He looked away and continued walking toward the front door.

Blair took a moment to see the place through his eyes. It was rustic on the outside, intentionally built that way to blend in with nature. Nothing but logs and wood finish. Even the porch was made of logs. The porch swing too. It swayed slightly in the wind as she followed Dade.

He leaned against the log siding as she unlocked the door and then opened it. The alarm beeped, and she turned to the panel to disarm it. After flipping on the lights, she stepped out of the way. "Home sweet home."

Dade followed her inside, shutting the door behind him. "We didn't bring a thing with us." He frowned.

She kept walking through the front room, opening the curtains and then adjusting the thermostat. "Ryan dropped off everything you'll need yesterday. He stocked the guest room with clothes and whatever shit men need." She shot him a grin, trying to lighten the mood.

He was going to be a tough man to crack. And she was assuredly not the right person to do the job. Her experiences with men were limited. Mostly they never lived up to her standards, so she didn't give them the time of day. Or maybe no one could *ever* live up to her standards. The walls around her heart were high.

She had dated some when she was younger, but she'd found that a woman who joined the army right out of high school was looked at differently most of the time.

She didn't care what other people thought. She had been a bitter, damaged, angry teenager. Joining the army had been the best thing she could have done for herself. It had turned her into someone she was proud of. After serving her country for ten years, she never looked back with regret.

"Why did you agree to this?" Dade asked, shocking her.

She headed for the kitchen next, pondering how she wanted to answer his question. She wasn't completely sure what to tell him.

She wasn't even sure if she knew the answer. She peered in the fridge to find it fully stocked. That was good. Not that she doubted Ryan.

Finally, she turned around and leaned against the counter, crossing her legs at the ankles and meeting Dade's intense stare. "It's my job. I'm good at it. I've been on protection detail for a lot of people in the last seventeen years."

"Huh, you don't look old enough to have served that long."

"I get that a lot. I'm thirty-five. I joined right out of high school. Served ten years. Got out. Took a job at the bunker. Been there seven years. Pretty boring resume."

He nodded. "I doubt that. I would have put you closer to thirty. We're the same age, then. Technically."

"Which is strange since you were born a decade before me. I'm still getting used to all you people waking up in bodies that have not aged."

She decided to elaborate a bit while he wandered around her living space, taking in what she had perfected over the years. "I was in the room with Ryan and Emily when Ryan realized you were not going to be able to receive the cure for AP12. In order to keep the details of your existence and whereabouts limited to as few people as possible, it was logical to assign me to protect you."

"I see." He didn't look at her, but kept wandering. He picked up various items and set them back down, but she didn't think he really saw them.

"Come on. I'll show you the rest." She shoved off the counter and spread her arm. "Kitchen, of course. I changed very little about the cabin when I bought it. I fell in love with the modern simplicity hidden in the rustic look of wood cabinets and floors and furniture. The previous owner sold it to me with the furniture included. I replaced a few things over the years, but most of it was already here."

He didn't respond.

She headed for the entrance to the hallway, pointing to the left as she arrived. "Master bedroom." She then pointed to the next door on the left and said, "Workout room." Across from it, she indicated, "Bathroom." And finally, first door on the right. "Guest bedroom. I'll let you have the master since the bed is king-sized. You'd be dwarfed in the smaller queen bed that's in the guest bedroom."

"You've never had a guest," he pointed out as he entered the smaller room.

"True. I also have no idea what that mattress is like. The sheets are clean, but beyond that, I guess I'll find out."

"You won't. I can manage a queen-sized bed. You're not giving up your room." He opened some of the drawers on the dresser and closed them. "Besides, Ryan put things in here for me. It would be ridiculous to switch."

"Okay. But I offered. If it's not comfortable, let me know. We can order another mattress or—"

He interrupted her. "It'll be fine. You're not replacing the mattress in a bedroom no one uses for a man who's dying." He walked past her, through the front room, and back out the front door.

Well, shit.

CHAPTER 5

Dade had wandered around the perimeter of the cabin for almost half an hour before he headed back toward the front door. He needed to get a grip on himself before he said things he couldn't take back. He lifted his face to the clear sky and inhaled the clean air. Too bad he wasn't going to be on this earth very long to enjoy it. The weight of that realization sank in deeper. So was the fact that he was being an asshole about it.

It wasn't Blair's fault he was dying. The woman was doing everything in her power to be kind and helpful. She had given up every second of free time she normally had to bring his sorry ass to her private getaway. He needed to be grateful and stop being a dick.

In another life, he would have found her attractive. She was petite but fierce. Strong in body and soul. She didn't wear much makeup or other girly things, but she didn't need it. If she let her hair down, literally, so that it fell over her shoulders, she would be more feminine than nearly everyone he'd seen since he woke up.

He couldn't decide if she hid her curvy body and gorgeous hair from the world on purpose, or if she didn't know she possessed such charms.

Exhaustion was tugging at him. He hadn't walked that far or even stood that long in the two weeks he'd been reanimated. Mostly because he'd been out of sorts even before Ryan dropped his bombshell.

He didn't have family to contact, and his closest friends were still preserved in cryostats. He would have loved to have had the chance to reacquaint with Tushar and Trish, but he understood why they hadn't been at the bunker too. Their safety was important.

The few friends Dade had maintained from childhood would be ten years older than him now with completely different lives. Families even. He feared it would depress him to make contact with any of them, which was fine since Temple had impressed upon him the need to remain completely silent.

Maybe Blair was right. Maybe he needed to stop acting like an ass and enjoy his remaining days. So far he'd treated her rather unkindly, but she didn't seem like the sort of person who would punish him for his behavior forever.

Did he want to open up to her and start a friendship, though? He wasn't really in the mood for forging new relationships. They took effort and time to cultivate. He didn't have the energy for the former or the remaining days for the latter.

A loud noise caught his attention as he reached the house, and he turned to the left to round the cabin, adrenaline pumping. It didn't take long to find the source of the racket.

Blair stood in the small clearing behind the cabin, her back to him, a hatchet in the air. She was chopping wood.

He grabbed the side of the house and watched as she swung again, splitting the log down the center before reaching down to drop the axe and pick up the pieces.

When she turned around, she startled. "Hey. I was worried about you." She continued toward the back of the cabin and dropped the pieces in her hand on a tall pile.

He felt like an even larger ass. "I was wandering the perimeter.

Let me help you." He stepped closer, unable to fathom in his wildest dreams how he was going to help her in his current state of weakness, but there wasn't a chance in hell he was going to watch a woman chop wood to keep him warm. He didn't even recognize himself.

She smiled. "I got it. Go on inside and warm up. It's getting colder out here."

He glanced at the tall pile by the back door. "You don't think we have enough wood?"

"We have plenty, but it's supposed to start snowing in a few hours, and you never know how deep it might get or how long it might last. If I don't have anything else to do, I always take advantage of breaks in the weather during the winter to make sure I'm prepared."

As she turned back around to pick up the hatchet and another log, he lurched forward, grabbing her wrist.

She flinched, her gaze meeting his, inches separating them. Her face was flushed. From the cold or his proximity? Her eyes were wide. "What?"

"Drop the axe and go inside before you so totally emasculate me to the point that I won't be able to look in a mirror."

Her breath hitched. She licked her lips. Her cheeks turned a darker pink. "That's not my intention, Dade."

"I know," he whispered. "But it's your result." He'd never been this close to her. He could smell her shampoo and the body soap she used combined with her own personal scent. He was surprised to catch a whiff of something floral or fruity. He wouldn't have expected that.

"It's just wood, Dade. I've been chopping my own wood for four years without help." Her voice was thready, raw, pitched lower than usual. Dare he think sexy?

Shaking that thought from his head, he continued. "I get that, but please humor me. I'll make you a deal. You put that hatchet away for today. There's obviously enough wood already chopped for weeks of bad weather. And your cabin has heat too. In exchange, I promise to get stronger so I can take over the task."

He had no idea why he was proposing such a thing. Moments ago he had considered climbing into that queen-sized bed with not a single care in the world for how old the mattress was and sleeping until he died. Why the hell had he just agreed to work out and get healthy?

Because he hadn't been raised to sit around lounging while a woman did all the hard work. That's why.

"Okay. Deal." Her soft voice reached inside him and tugged. Her smile melted another chunk of his frozen soul. Ironic, since the only part of him that had not actually been "frozen" for the last ten years should have been his soul.

When she lifted her other hand to cup his face, her fingers melted another piece. He really needed to walk away before his mind wandered into forbidden territory.

Until this moment, he hadn't put a single second of thought into his primal needs since waking up two weeks ago. Suddenly, parts of him that had lain dormant for ten years came to life. Probably because Blair was the only woman around for miles and miles. Probably because he'd gone through a long dry spell even before his preservation. Probably because she wasn't hard on the eyes and she smelled so good.

He dropped her wrist and stepped back, breaking contact. Without another word, he spun around and headed into the cabin and straight through to the guest bedroom. His heart was racing, and he could still feel the tips of her fingers on his cheek as he shut the door and then flopped down on the bed.

Deep breaths. This was not good.

This was so, so not good.

～

Not surprisingly, Dade fell asleep. When he woke up, it was to the smell of food. Not just food, but he was almost certain the scent was hamburgers. His stomach growled. He hadn't had lunch, and a glance at the window told him it was dark out and snowing heavily.

He shoved himself to sitting, hating how his body betrayed him with its refusal to operate at 100 percent. If nothing else, he didn't want to spend the rest of his life unable to complete the simplest of tasks. He wanted his body back. The one that could climb mountains.

As he pushed to his feet, he turned around and stared at the bed. Yep, the mattress was too soft. He'd been too tired to notice when he came into the room, and he'd flopped onto his back and fallen asleep quickly. But now that he was more alert, he had to smirk. *Maybe I should have taken her up on the offer to switch rooms.* His back ached from sinking too low.

The moment he stepped into the great room, his suspicion was confirmed. Definitely burgers.

Blair lifted her gaze and smiled. "Hey, I hope I didn't wake you. I was trying to be quiet, but you have to be starving. Did you sleep well?"

"Like a rock."

"Is the mattress okay?"

"It's fine," he lied. He set his hands on the heavy country table in the center of the room to brace himself. He'd moved too fast. He was dizzy. "You cook too?"

She chuckled, the sweetest little sound that made his spine tingle. "No. I'm a terrible cook. I'm much better at chopping wood." Her blue eyes danced with laughter when she looked at him. "I might have pulled a bait and switch luring you to my cabin." She winced intentionally. "After a few meals, you'll probably want to hunt squirrel or something instead. I'm much better with a frozen dinner than a knife and cutting board."

He lowered onto the closest chair. "It's your lucky day, then.

My grandparents raised me, and my grandmother thought any proper husband should know how to cook, so she taught me everything. I can even make biscuits from scratch without a recipe. If my brain is able to pull it up after hibernating, that is."

Her eyes widened. "Blessed angels. When are you going to make those biscuits? My mouth is watering."

He laughed. *Laughed?* What was this woman doing to him?

When she turned back around to face the stove, he watched her every move. She had changed into some sort of skintight black workout pants and a well-worn navy-blue sweatshirt with the neck and the sleeves cut so that it hung off her shoulders. On second thought, he decided the shirt was probably purchased to look like that. If he wasn't mistaken, she had on a black sports bra, one strap of which was visible on her shoulder.

His gaze didn't linger there, however, because her ass was so prominently featured in those damn pants that no man would be able to avoid staring. There was no way she had anything on underneath them either.

Jesus. He jerked his gaze to his hands on the table when she turned around. "You like cheese on your maybe-raw, maybe-burnt burger?"

"Yes." She could do anything she wanted to those burgers as long as she wore that outfit to cook in.

What the hell was he thinking? This woman was not here for him to ogle. And she certainly hadn't brought him to her home so he could fuck her. Was he even capable of sex? The fact that he had to adjust his jeans under the table spoke volumes. Plus, surely Ryan would have mentioned something if the other three had awakened without all parts working. After all, his parents were off in Montana reconnecting.

She set several items on the other side of the table. It was a high-top that he surmised had to function as a work surface also because there wasn't enough other counter space, and the thick wooden table was in the center of the room.

In fact, the chair that belonged in that particular spot at the table had been removed and leaned against the far wall as if she had placed it there years ago and never bothered to put it back. Why would she need it if she lived here alone?

He watched her intently as she sliced a tomato and prepared lettuce. "I wasn't sure if I should warn you about my cooking skills, or lack thereof. You're super lucky I can even make burgers. I have about three staples. Other than that, I'm helpless."

"So we were going to eat three meals, and then you were going to drop the bomb?" he teased.

"More or less, but then I chickened out."

"Have you ever been married?" he asked without thinking. What a dumb question.

She shook her head and grinned. "You were wondering if I might bother telling anyone I couldn't cook before the ceremony, weren't you?"

He shrugged.

"I'm not that sadistic. I wouldn't want to harm anyone. But for the average kidnap victim I bring back to the cabin, I guess I don't have to list my culinary credentials."

"Kidnap victim, huh?"

"I get the feeling that's how you see yourself." She set the plate of fixings in the middle of the table and turned around to the stove again. Two seconds later, she flipped off the burner and brought the pan to the table to set it on the potholder in the middle.

After grabbing a bag of buns and some sodas, she had everything tossed on the table and took a seat at an angle next to him. When she slid a plate in front of him, he set his hand on hers, forcing her to meet his gaze. "Sorry I've been such a dick. It's not your fault I'm in this mess. I shouldn't take it out on you. I'm still trying to wrap my head around the facts."

She put her other hand on top of his, trapping his fingers. "It's okay. We don't even know each other. You were thrust into a situation without your say so. I get it. We'll figure things out. One day at a time."

When she released his hand, he felt the loss of her warmth. Her braid fell over one shoulder again. It was cute. It made her look younger than thirty-five.

Dade went to work doctoring his burger and then took a tentative bite. It was delicious. "Mmm. Perfect," he murmured around the first mouthful. After he swallowed he said, "You lie."

She chuckled, swallowing her own first bite. "I got lucky this time. Trust me."

He did trust her. For one thing, if Ryan, Emily, and Temple trusted her, then he would never doubt her. That didn't mean he liked this arrangement any better than he had five minutes ago, but at least she was a likeable person and not hard on the eyes.

"Tell me about your grandparents," she began after a few more bites. "Where were your parents?"

"They died when I was young. I don't remember them. Freak accident. They owned a jewelry store in a strip mall. The store below them caught fire. They were trapped and died of smoke inhalation."

"Oh, God. I'm so sorry."

He shrugged. "Like I said, I was too young to remember."

"So your grandparents raised you?"

"Yep." He swallowed another bite of burger and wiped his lips. "My grandmother died when I was fifteen. My grandfather was heartbroken. It was difficult. There wasn't money for me to go to college, so I entered the army to pay for my degree, and then got assigned to Project DEEP. The rest you know."

He was surprised by his ability to open up to her. He rarely would have shared these kinds of details with anyone before he got sick ten years ago, the first time. Emily wasn't wrong when she described him. He had been a kidder back then. Always cracking jokes. Making people laugh. A psychiatrist would probably say it helped him bury the pain of losing so many people. He was intelligent enough to figure that out.

"I thought Ryan said you had no living relatives. When did your grandfather pass?"

"Three years ago." He looked away. That part was the most painful. It would have helped if he could have awoken to find at least that one connection still existed for him.

"I'm sorry. That must have been hard to find out."

"Yes." He took a breath, sat up straighter, and shook off the melancholy. "Enough about me. Tell me about you. I have visions of four brothers who roughhoused with you for your entire childhood so that you became tough and domineering."

She laughed, pushing her plate away. "Hate to disappoint you, but not even close. I only had one sister. No brothers at all."

"Had?"

"Yeah, she died when I was sixteen. But my parents are still living. They live in Florida now, enjoying retired life."

He didn't miss the way she glossed over her sister's death and moved on. It seemed prudent to let that subject go. "What made you enter the army?"

"Same as you. There wasn't enough money, so I joined right out of high school. But I found the military suited me, so I stayed ten years."

He leaned back in his chair and watched her intently as she spoke. She was leaving some parts out intentionally. That much he was sure of. Why did she leave the army after ten years of service? It was none of his business. He was her guest. Digging around in her personal life was not appropriate. So, he changed the subject. "Tell me where you keep weapons around here so I'll know in an emergency." It seemed far-fetched that anyone could find the cabin, especially after he had walked the periphery. They were well and truly off the beaten path.

"Right." She stood, grabbing their plates. "I'll clean this up and then show you my hiding places."

He stood next to her, taking the plates from her hand. "I'll clean up. You cooked."

She cocked her head to one side and released the plates. "Not going to turn that down. The only thing worse than cooking is cleaning."

He glanced around. "The place is immaculate. You obviously clean it often."

"I didn't say I *don't* clean. I just said I didn't like it. You'll find I'm a bit quirky. A little anal, some people say. I don't fit the mold of your average woman. I beat to my own drum." After dropping that completely cryptic information, she left him standing there holding the plates.

He watched her ass again as she headed for her bedroom, assuming she went to get something. In her absence, he loaded everything in the dishwasher and started the machine. When he turned around, he found her returning. She held out a Glock. "You can have this one, as long as you promise you won't shoot me or yourself."

He started to chuckle, but stopped himself. She was dead serious. As he took it from her hands, he met her gaze. "I would never do either. I promise I'm not that unstable. Not right now anyway. I'll admit I'm furious at what life has dealt me, but I'm not at a point where I would kill myself."

She nodded. "If you find yourself changing your mind, you better fucking tell me, because I swear to God, Dade, I will hunt your ass down and kill you a third time if you commit suicide on my watch."

He set the Glock on the table and stepped closer. She was flushed. Her hands were shaking. When he reached out to touch her wrist, she stepped back. "Let me show you everything else," she said, turning away.

He had no idea what the hell just happened between them, but holy fuck. Instead of commenting, he followed her. Ten minutes later, he had a handle on every weapon she owned, where they were located, and where she kept extra ammunition. He also learned how to arm and disarm the alarm.

"This is like a fortress," he stated. "Why so much protection if you've never even brought anyone here you were guarding?"

She shrugged again. She did that a lot. He was coming to realize it was her way of saying *none of your business*. Her words never quite matched. "I'm careful."

Again. Super informative.

CHAPTER 6

Blair had mixed feeling about the last hour. On the one hand, she was glad Dade was showing signs of life. On the other hand, he had gotten really personal. She wasn't the sort of person who opened up like that. It had been a long time since she even had a friend she was close enough with that she would share intimate details.

Since her harrowing incident with Emily six months ago, the two of them had bonded and become friends. Nevertheless, Blair still hadn't shared her deepest secrets with her newly reanimated friend.

Emily was...easy. She didn't ask for more than Blair was willing to share. She listened intently, loved fiercely, and spoke her heart. Blair actually felt guilty for the unbalance in their relationship sometimes.

And then there was Dade.

As she settled into the depths of her favorite comfy chair to stare at and enjoy the fire and attempt to escape into a book, she found herself watching him move around her home.

It was weird having another person in her private space, especially one she knew very little about. It was like he was getting to know her through her things. She didn't mind, but she was unnerved.

Sometimes he got the most serious look on his face. It was usually followed with personal questions she wasn't willing to answer. She guarded her heart tight—not just from men but from all people. It was probably the reason she'd never entered a serious relationship.

She liked being alone. It was safe. She couldn't get hurt if she never got close enough to anyone for them to disappoint her. For many years that decision hadn't been conscious, and then one day another female coworker pointed it out to her as if she were a mind reader.

Blair had pondered the woman's words for days before realizing she had been right. Blair was closed off from any real meaningful human interaction. It was for a good reason, but that didn't make it healthy. Since then, she had managed to develop deeper friendships, Emily among them, but she still hadn't let men get too close to her.

When Dade settled on the couch, he pointed out the obvious. "You don't have a television."

"Nope. When I'm here, I like to be with nature. I like to read. Relax. Enjoy my surroundings. Television doesn't seem like it has a place here."

He nodded, his lips curving up slightly in that look of appreciation and understanding. "Makes sense. I like it."

"I have all kinds of books on the shelves if you want grab one."

He glanced around at the built-in shelves she had flanking the fireplace and on the opposite wall behind the couch. "Anything from the last ten years?"

"Most of my stuff is from the last ten years." As soon as the words left her mouth, she realized what he meant.

He smiled again. "Then I shouldn't have any trouble finding something I haven't read."

A flush crossed her face for no reason. It wasn't as though she'd made a huge social blunder, but it felt like it.

He leaned his head back and stared at the ceiling. "You have a computer, right? Ryan said there was internet."

"Yes. I'll be happy to give you a quick tutorial to bring you up to speed. You can use it all you want. I have unlimited data."

He nodded, still staring at the ceiling as if it had answers, or perhaps questions. "I've heard about your internet speed these days, and Emily mentioned you can literally look up anything in the world you want and get thousands of sources on any topic. My curiosity is piqued."

"It's true. It happened so fast that I can't even remember what it was like before we had the world at our fingertips. Music too. Anything you want to listen to, we can find it."

He sighed. "Don't introduce me to too many things. It will just make it that much harder to give them up."

The way he worded that was disturbing. As if he would be moving to a desert island instead of dying. In death, she didn't imagine he would be aware of what he was missing.

She shook her head to clear her mind of the morbid thoughts. He mentioned his death so often that she had to repeatedly remind herself of two facts: He wasn't actively dying as he liked to proclaim, and there existed the possibility someone would find a cure before it was too late.

She wondered how many people in the world were suffering from diseases that were on the cusp of being cured. Waiting. Hoping. Holding their breath.

Dade wasn't one of those people because so far, he had not even touched on the possibility of hope. He had dismissed any chatter about possible treatments out of hand and had been morbidly focused for the last two days on his doom.

Even though his attitude had softened throughout the day, until he was no longer scowling and throwing a toddler-sized tantrum, he still had shown no signs he had any hope.

She fully intended to cure him of that unhealthy state of mind, as much for her own sanity as his. It would be depressing to spend weeks or even months with a man who refused to embrace life.

Yeah, she was in uncharted territory. She had taken this on of her own free will. Someone had needed to step up to the plate, and she'd known it had to be her. Inviting another person into the fold would have increased the risk of a leak.

She also fully grasped the importance of saving Dade's life. If any member of the first team were to die, it could create a setback for the entire project. Future reanimations could be put on hold while further safety measures were ensured. Blair understood how unique Dade's situation was, as did Ryan and Emily and the other members of the new team, but would the government?

No scientist wanted progress to be halted. In fact, there were now four chambers actively working to reanimate more people at a time. Leaving the rest of the earlier team in limbo would bring bile to the throat of every scientist inside the bunker.

Blair had been involved from the start, finding out about Dade's condition by coincidence because of her proximity to Ryan when he discovered the earth-shattering truth. She had also been standing outside Dade's door yesterday morning on guard when he heard the news. She was trained to protect people. She owned a cabin.

It had been a no-brainer.

The stars had aligned and declared Blair the savior of the day. If she were lucky, maybe she could also save Dade from himself.

If I'm lucky.

Did he have to be so damn attractive? Even when he was angry, he was sexy. His hair was the sort women probably ran their hands through. His eyes were a deep brown that captivated her with their intensity every time he stared at her. Mesmerizing. Thoughtful. Deep.

If that was the way he looked at a woman when he had them in his arms, he surely had melted the hearts of a lot of lucky women.

And he was hers for the foreseeable future.

He's not yours, Blair. He's not a toy.

Yeah, she was going to need to keep her distance and hold her heart close to avoid falling for him. It was unsettling how he managed to unbalance her from the start. She never got rattled like that in front of a man.

Never.

And yet.

Dade Menke was going to put her through a lot of tests. She hoped she passed them all and came out on the other side intact. It was going to be a challenge.

A loud noise outside sent her scrambling to her feet in an instant.

Dade also jumped up.

They both rushed across the room at the same time, heading for the front window like a couple of stupid teenagers in a horror film. Blair hit the lights, leaving them in darkness except for the flickering of the fire. She hadn't closed the curtains, an oversight on her part.

She wasn't used to guarding someone in her home. She'd gotten lax this afternoon, let her guard down, assumed no one could find them in her cabin.

She set her hands on the window sill and peered into the night. Her heart was racing, but it was snowing so hard it was impossible to imagine anyone out there for any reason, not even bad intentions. At least eight inches of snow had fallen since that afternoon.

She could sense Dade at her back, his breath on her exposed skin. Warm.

Another loud crack sounded, the same as the first, like a gunshot.

Dade's hands were on her hips in a heartbeat, tugging her closer to the floor. "Jesus, woman. Get down."

She fought his tugging and jerked her attention in the

direction of the noise just as a branch broke free from a nearby tree and fell to the ground.

Dade must not have been facing the same direction because he continued to pull her away from the window. Finally, he wrapped an arm around her middle and yanked her to the floor, toppling forward enough that his chest slammed into her and pinned her against the wall beneath the window.

"Who the hell is protecting whom here?" he growled. "You're going to get us both killed."

His forearm rested under her breasts, brushing against them and making her far more aware of her body than she should be. Now that she knew they were in no danger, her attention shifted to every inch of her in contact with every inch of him.

For a man who'd spent a decade in a cryostat and hadn't done much of anything to regain his strength yet, his pecs were awfully firm.

The sports bra she was wearing wasn't thick enough to keep her nipples from reacting to his touch and jutting out to brush against the wall. It took her several seconds to find her voice, especially since he continued to wrestle her to the floor as if she were in serious danger of being shot at any second.

"Dade," she finally managed in a whisper.

"Shh." He had one hand on her head now, pressing her lower, and one hand on her waist, his fingers under her sweatshirt, resting against her bare skin.

She sucked in a breath. "Dade," she said louder this time. "It was a branch."

He stiffened. "What?"

"A branch. The tree a few yards from the left corner of the house died last summer. The weight of the snow is making the dead limbs snap." She waited for him to internalize her words and let her go.

He blew out a long breath, releasing his tight grip. "You're sure?"

"Yes. I watched the second one fall. It sounded exactly like a gunshot, but it was a branch." She didn't fight him, partially because she liked the feel of him against her. She shouldn't, but she did.

Slowly, he leaned back, bringing her with him, until he finally let her go, turned so that his back was to the front door, and dropped the last few inches to his ass.

He groaned and set his elbows on his knees, his face lowered. "Shit." He ran a hand through his hair.

Blair positioned herself next to him, taking deep breaths. "I thought we were under attack. That was so loud." She mostly said those words to reassure him he was not crazy for overreacting.

Dade said nothing. His breathing was heavier than hers.

She reached for his thigh to give him a reassuring squeeze. He stiffened, but otherwise didn't move. "Dade?"

"Yeah. Give me a second."

She removed her hand and closed her eyes, slowing her breathing as they sat there.

After a few minutes, he sat up straighter and turned to face her. "You have a death wish?"

"No." Really? He wanted to reprimand *her* now?

"Then why the hell did you run straight for the window? You could have gotten shot."

She stared into his eyes, seeing the fear that was manifesting as anger. "I would have shot back." She lifted the gun in her free hand.

His eyes went wider. "How did you manage to get over here with a weapon?"

She smiled. "I'm a trained professional."

He rolled his eyes. "You're a crazy woman."

"Well, I'm not going to deny that, but you don't have to worry about me, Dade. I'm a big girl. I've been in far worse situations than this one. Even if it had been a real threat."

He tipped his head toward the door. "Did you serve overseas?"

"Yes. Three tours."

He frowned. "In a PPD unit?"

"Yes." He remembered his acronyms. Personal protection detail had been her specialty.

"What kind of people?"

"Classified."

"Of course." He rolled his head back against the door and faced the room. "Why did you leave the army?"

"Honestly? My commanding officer was a dick. I couldn't take it anymore. Most of the people in the army treated me equally. And I worked my ass off to ensure that was the case. But not him. He was a misogynist. I was never going to win him over or be treated fairly. I finally decided I could make more money with less hassle in the private sector."

"Jesus. I'm so sorry, Blair." His brow was furrowed in anguish. "How many times have you been shot?"

She gave a low chuckle. "Worried about my abilities?"

"No. I have to acknowledge your competence. I'm just curious."

"Just the once. Six months ago with Emily." She shuddered, like she always did when she thought back on that moment last summer. "It wasn't pleasant. I vowed never to get shot again."

He chuckled this time. "Did you now?" The look he narrowed on her was his devastating one, the one he probably used to pick up women in bars. "Can I ask you something incredibly personal?"

"Yes, but I can't guarantee I'll answer it." She forced nonchalance in her voice even though her mind was racing with all the possibilities. She was not, however, prepared for his next question.

"Why aren't you married?"

She startled. That hadn't been what she expected.

"Never mind. That was too personal. I shouldn't have asked." He hesitated while she still tried to find a response. Then he continued. "It's just that you're so…" His voice trailed off and his face turned red. He shook his head and pushed to standing. "Ignore me."

I'm so what? He left that statement hanging with so many possibilities. She tipped her head back and watched him walk away until he disappeared into her guest bedroom.

After several moments, she managed to ease to her feet and head toward her own bedroom. After she shut the door, she leaned against it and sighed. She wasn't sure what to think of his question, or the fact that he hadn't given her a chance to answer. She wasn't sure she had wanted to answer or even knew the answer.

Was he interested in her? Or was he just curious? She wondered how he saw her. She had spent her adult life in the role of a badass woman. She knew she wasn't very feminine and didn't put off a vibe that attracted men. She did that on purpose. Put up walls. Kept people at arm's length. Especially men.

In the military, people expected that. With the exception of her commanding officer, they also respected it. There were some women in the army who flirted and dated and made their rounds, but not many, and she had never been one of them. She wore little makeup, kept her hair simple, and rarely put on a dress or skirt.

Her personality had been more of a tomboy even when she was young. Not because she didn't have a feminine side. She did. It was underneath the tough exterior. But after her world crumbled when she was only sixteen, she became bitter and hid from society the best way she knew how—baggy clothes, hoodies, and ponytails.

She grew tired of having teachers and other adults question her all the time. Was she okay? How was she doing? She wanted to be left alone. She wanted to fade into the background, unnoticed. It was easier.

Two years later, she joined the army right out of high school. It was the best decision she could have made, and she never regretted it. When she found herself on a path toward becoming the member of a personal security detail, her reputation as more badass than feminine solidified further.

It was the perfect job for her. Protecting people. Keeping people alive. She hadn't done such a bang-up job of it when she was young, but she found a way to do it as an adult.

Keeping other people safe had become a priority to her. It was more important than anything in the world. It fulfilled her in a way nothing else ever would. Including marriage or children. She didn't need a man, and she'd never been tempted by one either. Not even one she was charged with protecting. Until now. Until Dade.

Men mostly ignored her. And that was a good thing. She preferred it that way. Never let them get too close. Never let her heart get involved. It was safer. If she never let herself fall for anyone, they couldn't hurt her when they left. She'd lived with that motto running in her head for half her life. Never had there been a time when it was more fitting. As much as she hated to admit it to herself, there was a good chance Dade would leave her.

Unfortunately, Dade didn't seem inclined to ignore her. In fact, she'd caught him looking at her more than once. And she sighed as she remembered the feel of his arm wrapped protectively around her and then his body pressing against hers as he thought to protect her instead of the other way around.

It should have infuriated her. It normally would have. But this was Dade. Instead of bringing her down a rung and making her feel like she couldn't do her job, his touch felt way too good.

She sauntered toward her attached bathroom and turned on the hot water to fill the tub. A bath would soothe her. One of the luxuries of life she permitted herself even when time was a crunch.

She stripped out of her yoga pants, sweatshirt, and bra and stepped into the filling tub.

Yeah, she needed to get a grip on her reactions to Dade Menke.

She absolutely couldn't allow herself to fall for the man. It was the worst idea in the history of ideas.

She would keep her eyes off his body and her hands to herself. No more grabbing his hand or touching his chest. No more squeezing his thigh.

This was a serious job. She needed to be alert at all times, prepared for anything, not drooling over the man's broad chest and full lips. She'd stared at him enough. Show was over. Time to work.

CHAPTER 7

Dade was startled awake, as usual, in the early hours of the morning. He had never shut the blinds in his room because he preferred to be able to see out and at least note if it was night or day when he woke up.

It was still dark out this time. He confirmed that with a glance at the clock on the nightstand. He was wide awake, however, so he decided to make his way to Blair's workout room, hoping he wouldn't wake her.

He hadn't entered that room yet, so he had no idea what equipment she might have in there, but what little he *did* know about her suggested she probably had every piece of equipment known to mankind.

After rummaging around in the drawers and closet, he discovered Ryan had done a fantastic job of outfitting him with everything he would need. Surely he had some help. Emily? That would make sense since Emily at least knew Dade.

Dressed in gym shorts, a T-shirt, and new tennis shoes, he carefully opened his door and made his way down the short hallway. When he stepped in the doorway, he froze.

He wasn't the only one to have made this decision in the early hours of the morning. Blair was already in the room. And she took his breath away.

Her back was to him, and she was using a bar attached to the ceiling to do pull-ups. It was strategically placed facing the window, though he could see her face in the glass that acted like a mirror against the darkness of early morning.

She hadn't spotted him yet. Her eyes were squeezed shut and her mouth pursed as she continued to pull her chin up over the bar. How many reps had she done before he arrived?

What made him stop breathing, however, was her clothing choice—or lack thereof. She wore nothing but tight, black workout shorts, a black sports bra, and tennis shoes. Her thick blond hair was pulled up in a ponytail, swaying with every lift of her body.

She had the body of a temptress. He'd already suspected as much over the course of the last few days as he watched her gradual transformation from a security uniform to jeans and a thermal shirt to leggings and a sweatshirt to now this nearly complete lack of cover that left nothing to the imagination.

And by nothing, he meant *nothing*. Until now, he hadn't had the opportunity to see her chest. Even with her back to him, he could see the rise and fall of her breasts as she lifted. In the window, he didn't miss a thing.

Jesus. How did someone as petite as her and as fit as he knew she was have such amazing tits?

Finally, she dropped to the floor and turned around. She startled. Not surprising. "Shit. I didn't see you. Did I wake you?"

A heated flush covered his cheeks at being caught ogling her, though she made no mention of it. He shook his head. "No. I actually snuck in here quietly, hoping I wouldn't wake *you*. How many damn reps did you do?"

She chuckled. "I'll let you know when you're caught up. How about that?"

Oh, so she was going to taunt him into working out. It was

effective too. He smiled. "All right. How much do I have to bench press to catch up?" he joked.

She shrugged her shoulders high. "Guess you'll find out when you get there too."

He had to focus hard to keep his gaze on her face. Her exposed belly was rock hard without an ounce of fat. She was an incredibly gorgeous woman who would make any man drop to his knees. Which meant one of two things. Either she didn't know she was sexy as hell, so she did nothing to flaunt her assets. Or, she didn't want to attract anyone to her, so she normally hid her body. At this point he was inclined to go with number one since she seemed oblivious to her allure standing in front of him wearing so little, with sweat running temptingly between her breasts.

She had pointedly not answered his question last night, not that he'd given her a chance. It had been rude to ask, but the look on her face had made him think there was definitely a story behind her desire to remain single.

Oh yeah, she was completely unfazed by her lack of clothing or the effect it might be having on him. She did nothing to hide herself. She didn't even appear to have brought a T-shirt to the room.

In fact, she moved on to the next apparatus and started doing leg lifts. "You won't catch up to me on any equipment if you continue to stand in the doorway," she joked. Her lips were tucked between her teeth as she exerted herself, but the corners of her mouth were lifted in a barely hidden smile.

He forced himself to come fully into the room, thinking there was no way in hell he would accomplish much as long as she was in there with him. She was going to be a distraction like none he'd ever experienced.

He grabbed a hand towel from a stack she had on a table in the corner and headed for her treadmill. He needed to learn to walk before he could run. There was no reason to be embarrassed about how bad of shape he was in after ten years of vitrification.

Nevertheless, he didn't intend to slack off around her for one more minute. If her goal in bringing him here had been to encourage him to get fit, she had succeeded. If she thought she might be able to tempt him into a competition by running around the house in that damn outfit…she had also succeeded.

He forced himself not to glance her direction as he turned on the machine. If he allowed himself to look at her, he would end up on the floor at the end of the treadmill with his head slamming into the conveyor belt.

He started walking at a fast clip, gradually increasing the speed without noticing she had come up beside him. Her voice made him grab the handles to keep from sliding off the end. "Slow down. This isn't a contest."

He smirked. "I thought you were pretty clear that it actually *is* a contest."

She stepped in front of him and set her hands on her hips. "Okay, big guy, but there isn't a prize for reaching your goals faster than what your body can handle. Take your time."

This was when he noticed the quarter-sized scar on her left biceps. He tried not to think about her getting shot and shifted his gaze to her face. "Don't you have some other equipment to fondle?" He nodded toward the bench. "Perhaps some sit-ups or something?"

"Fondle?"

"Yeah, well, you obviously love to work out, so I'm betting you have a pretty intimate relationship with every apparatus." What the hell was he doing teasing her like this?

She laughed. "You're not wrong." She walked away, leaving his mouth dry, wondering what the hell she meant by that. No way was he going to ask, though. He'd probably swallow his tongue if she got more specific. As it was, he couldn't keep from picturing her masturbating with her legs spread open either straddling the bench or forced apart by the leg machine.

He pursed his lips and stared straight ahead, increasing the speed of the treadmill so that he started his first slow jog. He had a long way to go, but he intended to get there if it took every last day of his short life.

Yeah, if her goal had been to entice him to get in shape so he could enjoy the rest of his numbered days, she had definitely succeeded. Game on.

～

Two hours later, while Blair was in the shower, Dade made his way to her kitchen. He took a few minutes to get the lay of the land, and then he pulled out all the ingredients for omelets and hash browns. He had bacon frying and was chopping vegetables when she wandered in.

Her hair was wet and hanging down her back. He'd never seen it down since he met her. It was longer than he expected. She had on another pair of those damn tight, black legging things. She also wore a fitted, long-sleeved, lime-green sports shirt. This time she was not hiding her chest.

He nearly cut his finger off as he forced his gaze back to the cutting board.

"That smells amazing. I hit the jackpot. If I had known you could cook, I might have kidnapped you two weeks earlier." She set her elbows on the high-top table across from him and leaned forward, not helping matters at all with her breasts thrust forward and pressed together.

He attempted to laugh at her joke.

Did the woman have any idea what she was doing to him?

He gritted his teeth and turned away as if he needed to check the bacon that very second.

He knew several things. One, his body was fully functional.

Two, he wasn't going to last another full day without her figuring that out. Three, he wasn't going to last long inside the confined space alone with her and her scent without taking her.

Was it possible his attraction was based solely on the fact that she was the only woman around and the first person to tempt him since he woke up two weeks ago?

He glanced over his shoulder and nixed that idea in a hurry. She was fucking hot. She either didn't know it or didn't care—both of which made her even more attractive.

It wasn't really a matter of opinion. It was a fact. He wasn't so far removed from society that he couldn't see she was a strong, sexy woman—qualities he found appealing.

Part of him rationalized there was no reason to spend the rest of his numbered days living like some kind of monk while there was a fantastic tempting woman within reach. He couldn't do that to her, of course. It wouldn't be fair. But, God, how he wanted to turn around, grab her sexy body by the waist, set her on the counter, and fuck the daylight out of her.

It was important to remind himself that he was her guest. She was doing him a favor. It would be inappropriate and rude as fuck to come on to her. It could also ruin their tenuous relationship as friends. She'd brought him here to keep him safe from the rest of the world. Did she have any idea how very unsafe he was from *her*?

"Looks like it finally stopped snowing," he said to fill the silence.

"Yep. But we got more than a foot, and it's supposed to start again later tonight." She shoved off the table and walked over to the back door to look out.

He blew out a breath. At least her tits were no longer in his face. Of course, her ass was almost worse, and it was on display. He would be subjected to one or the other at all times. Couldn't she put on some more damn clothes?

He sautéed the vegetables for several minutes and then poured the eggs over them. The potatoes were almost done, and the bacon was draining on a paper towel. "So, you have a computer I can use, right?"

She turned around. "Yes. I'll set it up for you after we eat. I usually work at the kitchen table. The modem is on the counter." She pointed to the black box he hadn't noticed behind the phone.

"Probably going to need a tutorial of your latest computer updates and internet usage if they're anything like your weird phone apps and that iPad thing."

She giggled, a sound he was beginning to enjoy a bit too much. "I have an iPad too if you need it."

He shook his head rapidly as if clearing it of the clutter that was 2018. "The world jumped ahead a hundred years while I slept for ten."

"Pretty much."

He filled their plates and set them on the table. "Let's eat." He took a deep breath as he slid onto the stool. He was going to have to get a grip on his absurd lust for this woman fast. If not, he would make a complete fool of himself before the end of the day. And this was only day two.

While he ate, he reminded himself that he wasn't available for any sort of relationship even if Blair or any other woman were game. He was going to die.

Ryan had been vague about his prognosis, so now that Dade had renewed energy, the first thing he intended to do was go through all of Ryan's data and notes to come up with his own diagnosis. Instead of continuing to wallow in self-pity, he could at least be useful to the other members of the team. What if someone else was revived with the same condition?

Above all, he was first and foremost a scientist. He had devoted his entire life to finding the cures for diseases. That devotion had included the virus he himself had succumbed to ten years ago. AP12. He needed to stop whining about his impending death and start looking for a cure for the deadly combination of

AA2 and AP12. If he couldn't find a treatment in time to save himself, at least he could move the research that much closer to keeping someone else alive in the future.

Suddenly realizing he was in his own world, he lifted his gaze to find Blair leaning back on her stool, arms crossed under her chest, staring at him intently. Her plate was empty. So was his for that matter.

She gave him a small smile. "You get really intense when you're thinking. What's been going on in that head of yours?"

At least that hadn't changed. "Yeah, I've been told that a time or two. I get inside my head and zone out the rest of the world. Everything else ceases to exist."

"Did you solve the mysteries of the universe while you were in there?"

"Not yet, but I did plot out a time frame for when I would like to have them all solved," he joked as he slid off the stool and took their plates to the sink.

"I'll clean up. You better get started saving the world." She followed him, taking the plates from his hands and setting them on the counter. "Let me get the computer so you can work, then I'll tackle this kitchen."

He nodded, grateful that she understood him without words.

Ten minutes later, he had his hand on her mouse and was exploring the internet. He was impressed to find that he could access any file Ryan shared with him and that Ryan had already set up a shared folder and included enough files to keep Dade busy for weeks.

The next time Dade had any cognizant knowledge of the universe was when a hand landed on his shoulder and a feminine body brushed against his side. He tipped his head toward Blair. "You've been working for hours. Why don't you take a break? You need to eat. You should walk around some."

He glanced at the window. "Shit. What time is it?"

"After five. The sun sets pretty early here this time of year."

He swiped a hand down his face and leaned back, aware of every one of her fingers still touching him. "Wow."

She slid onto the stool next to him. "What are you working on so intently?"

"Mostly I'm just adding to my frustration, to be honest. There have been so many advances in medicine in the last ten years that it's going to take me weeks just to catch up. Maybe months. I don't have months." He wasn't kidding. His stress level had skyrocketed the more he learned. Or rather the more he found out he needed to learn.

"I know it's in your genetic make-up to find a cure for diseases, but you can't fix everything in one day."

She had no concept of what he was facing. "I don't intend to fix *everything*, just AA2. And the clock is ticking."

She nodded slowly. "I understand."

"Do you?" He didn't mean to get snarky, but she was standing too close to him, touching him, her scent wafting toward him. He needed to put some distance between them before he grabbed her by the face and kissed her senseless.

Shoving the laptop closed, he slid off the other side of his stool and broke the contact, padding from the room. As soon as he was in the guest room, he shut the door and leaned against it. He had no idea why he'd been so sharp with her. There was no reason for it. She'd done nothing to deserve it.

Except be sexy in his space, which he couldn't deal with. He had work to do. She was the one who encouraged him to pull his shit together and live life to its fullest. What he hadn't anticipated was intense attraction to her. And now he had a problem.

He'd only known her three days, and that was a stretch if he counted their limited interaction the first day. How could he possibly fall for a woman he'd spent so little time with?

He headed for the window and peered out into the night. When deep breaths didn't calm him down, he opened the window a few inches, hoping the cold air would shock his system back to normal.

Whatever normal was.

He needed a new normal. He needed a routine. Exercise. Cook. Eat. Research. That was what his routine looked like *before* he was vitrified. He could return to some semblance of *that* normal again now.

Except before he'd gotten sick, he had spent his days in the bunker.

And there most certainly hadn't been a gorgeous woman wandering around in his space while he worked.

Dade needed to get his head on straight and focus. He had done enough research all day to better understand what he was facing.

First of all, Ryan and Emily were correct. There was no way of knowing how much time he had before he developed symptoms of AP12. Could be weeks. Could be months. With the total blood replacement, he had more time than someone else, and there certainly hadn't been anyone else battling AA2 who'd received a total blood replacement.

Fact number two, as soon as he received the shot that was meant to cure AP12, AA2 would kick into high gear and kill him within a month. That was not an option.

Fact number three, there were a number of drugs that had been developed to prolong the lives of people with AP12 before the cure had been discovered. When Dade started getting symptoms, he could start a treatment plan that would buy him some time. Months probably.

Meanwhile, the clock was ticking on making a decision. There were two possible paths that could save his life. One was the development of a cure for AA2. The other was a bone marrow transplant. The success rate of the transplant was less than 50 percent. Not good odds, but certainly a possibility if all else failed.

He could get on the donor registry list, but that would create an entire new pile of issues since his reanimation and existence were not public yet, and no one involved in the project wanted anyone to find out the reanimation of one of the team members had not been 100 percent successful. That would simply add fuel to the protesters and possibly stall the reanimation of the rest of the team.

Frankly, a bone marrow transplant was not at the top of Dade's list of fun things to do anyway.

Realizing he was cold, he pushed the window closed and lowered to the floor. His back hurt from hunching over Blair's computer all day after sleeping on that horrible mattress last night.

When a knock sounded at his door, he stiffened.

"Dade? You need to eat."

"I'll be out in a minute." He needed to regroup and find a way to face her because one thing was certain above all else—he was stuck with her in this small cabin for an indeterminate length of time. He needed to find a way to tamp down his weird lust and focus on saving his life. Because the last thing he should do was cross a line with her and risk making this entire adventure far more uncomfortable than it already was.

CHAPTER 8

Blair tossed and turned for most of the night. Visions of Dade hunched over that computer all day made her uneasy. His frustration was evident every few minutes by his growls. He had scribbled so many notes that he'd used up half a notebook. She would need to get him more paper if he intended to keep working at that pace.

Was it good for him? It probably wasn't any of her business, nor would she be able to keep him from researching the disease that was slowly killing him. She had brought this on herself in a way. After all, she'd encouraged him to find the will to live and stop moping. She couldn't very well expect him to paste on a smile and throw snowballs.

Nope. If he had the incentive to find a cure, he was the sort of person who would dive in and do the work himself. He was ten years behind on any medical research, so she was certain half his frustration stemmed from that impediment.

She tried not to let it bother her that he'd snapped at her and walked out of the room. He had a right to his permanent state of agitation. She couldn't blame him. She couldn't imagine how she would feel in his shoes.

Dragging herself out of bed, she decided to head for her home gym early again. At least working out cleared her mind. Maybe she could exhaust herself enough to get some sleep later. A nap would be wonderful. After the night she'd had worrying about Dade, she was going to be a zombie in a few hours.

When she entered the workout room, she wasn't surprised to find Dade already inside. He had once again been so quiet that she never heard him get up, but it was clear once the man set his mind to something, he did it. And getting fit had obviously been top on his list.

"Hey," she said, as she stepped into the room.

He was sitting on the leg machine, and he lifted his head to meet her gaze. "Hey. Did I wake you?"

She smiled. "Didn't we have this same conversation yesterday in reverse?"

He lifted a brow.

"No. You didn't wake me. You're like a mouse. Except when you're being a mad scientist." She hoped she could lighten the air around them, though she wasn't sure he could take a joke yet.

He stood, grabbing his hand towel and wiping his face. That moment gave her time to peruse his body. Damn. He was insanely built. He outweighed her by a lot, and he was nearly a foot taller. How long would she be able to outlift or outrun him? Both his stamina and his strength would be back in no time.

His pecs were so fine she couldn't imagine what they might be like in a few months. Suddenly, she realized she was fidgeting and her nipples were hard. In addition, he was staring at her, the towel dangling from his hand.

His expression gave nothing away as she jerked her gaze from him and rushed toward the treadmill. She too was going to get stronger and faster if she used this room to work out her growing sexual frustration. Had he seen her nipples through the sports bra? How embarrassing.

She started the machine and built up her speed quickly,

wanting to channel her energy so that a good sweat, flushed skin, and heavy breathing weren't the result of staring at the man who somehow filled every inch of her cabin.

He spoke from across the room. "Are you suggesting I make noises when I work?"

She shot him a glance, having almost forgotten her jab. "You could say that."

"I do not," he responded. "That's crazy." He wandered closer, which was not a good thing. She needed more space between them, not less. But it didn't stop him. Finally, his hand was on the front of the treadmill, and his eyes were penetrating hers. "I'm sorry I was so sharp last night. I was frustrated. It's going to happen a lot. I'll try not to take it out on you." His face went from serious to a slight smirk. "And I'll try to keep the noise down."

She stopped the treadmill to avoid falling while she spoke to him. Luckily, he kept his gaze on her face. If he glanced down, he would find her traitorous nipples still at attention. "Make all the noises you want. I don't mind. Though your mumbling is interesting. It's like you speak another language when you work."

He lifted a brow. "I talk?"

"Yes. Not intelligibly, but then again, I suppose it's possible that I wouldn't understand even if you were enunciating every word. I don't speak mad scientist."

He chuckled. Thank God. "Now you're going to give me a complex. How am I supposed to work, knowing you're watching me from across the room?"

"I could go outside and chop wood," she proposed. Their banter was easy and light. It felt natural.

"Don't even think about it. We have a deal."

"You'll never be able to hold up to your end of the bargain if you spend the morning standing there yapping. Get to work." She pointed at the free weights. "That axe is heavy," she joked.

He searched her eyes for several seconds, unnerving her with a look that seemed to climb into her soul to find out her secrets.

When she shuddered, he finally broke the stare and walked away. "I'll make breakfast when I finish here."

"Good because I'm spoiled now. I'll be expecting a four-course meal every morning."

He turned around as he picked up a weight. "I'll be happy to fix you breakfast if you'll do me the favor of setting a sandwich in my face at lunch. I tend to forget to stop and eat."

"I can do that." *See? Easy.* She could totally do this.

And then he bent over at the waist, accentuating his thighs and calves, and she nearly swallowed her tongue.

Stifling a groan, she jerked her attention to the window and turned the treadmill back on.

Shortly after noon, Blair's phone rang, and she answered the call quickly to keep from disturbing Dade. He was once again buried in work so thoroughly that she half expected to look up at some point and find he'd been sucked into the computer.

The screen told her it was Ryan. "Hey, Ryan."

"How are things?"

"Interesting," she responded. "I don't know what sort of research you've been working on for the last several months, but Dade is determined to double your efforts. He doesn't even come up for air when he's concentrating."

"Good. I mean, I'm glad to hear he's decided to care, but I hope he doesn't make himself crazy by overdoing it."

She was curled up in her favorite armchair, staring at the back of Dade's head while she spoke, fairly certain he had no idea she was even in the room, let alone speaking out loud. "Jury is still out on that."

He sighed. "Well, the reason I called is because my parents are back. I thought Dade might want to know. He can call them if he wants. It might help if he makes connections with people he knew ten years ago besides Emily and Temple. When this snow melts a bit, I'm sure they will want to come out there and visit."

"Is that wise?" Everyone was going to great lengths to ensure the cabin was a secret from the entire world. Every time someone came to visit, they ran the risk of being discovered.

"You're going to need supplies eventually. I'll smuggle in my mom and dad at the same time."

He was right about the supplies. And she knew for certain Tushar and Trish would never do anything to jeopardize Dade's safety. "How are they?" After the scare they had several days ago when someone found out their location on a remote ranch in Montana, she imagined they were pretty shaken up.

"They're good. My mom never wanted to leave here in the first place, so she's glad to be back. If I didn't know better, I'd say she was making up the entire story about two men chasing them down on that ranch just so she'd have an excuse to come back to the bunker."

Blair chuckled. She hadn't known either of his parents long, but what little she did know, told her he was undoubtedly speculating the truth. Trish had been formidable from the moment she woke up. Sending her away for her own safety had probably driven her mad.

Blair couldn't imagine being in the woman's shoes. If someone told Blair she had to hide out indefinitely from a madman, she might…

Shit. She squeezed her eyes shut as she realized that was exactly what Dade was experiencing.

"Well, I just wanted to check in," Ryan said. "Have Dade call anytime. I'll text you my parents' phone numbers."

"Sounds good. Thanks, Ryan." She ended the call, staring at the back of Dade's head and feeling the weight of what he was going through more thoroughly than she had since she met him.

Perhaps it might help if she made herself useful to him instead of sitting across the room reading an adventure novel. She didn't know shit about science, but she could at least gather data or something. Or help him research. Anything. Watching was not going to cut it.

Determined, she hauled herself out of the chair and padded across the room. He'd been weird all day around her. Quiet. Not making eye contact. If she didn't know better, she'd think he was suffering from the same affliction as her—lust. But that was crazy. He had a one-track mind. And rightfully so.

He was *not* thinking about her. At least not in that way.

She was nervous about interrupting him, but he needed to eat anyway, and he'd specifically asked her to hand him a sandwich. So, she went to work making lunch and then brought two plates over to the table.

Throughout all of that—the phone call and her making lunch —he never showed any sign he noticed she was even in the cabin. Hell, he didn't show any sign he realized that *he* was in the cabin.

"Dade." She gently touched his shoulder after setting the two plates on the table.

He jerked his gaze to her, unseeing for a moment. And then he blew out a breath, leaned back in his chair, and wiped a hand down his face. "Sorry. How long were you standing there?"

She smiled as she removed her hand. "Not long, but you really do zone out. Did you even hear me on the phone?"

He shook his head. "No. Sorry. I get distracted when I work. If you need my attention, you'll have to get in my face."

"Yeah, I don't think I'm going to do that. I'm afraid you'll take a swing at me." She was only half joking. When someone was that focused, it could be hazardous to anyone around to disrupt them.

One corner of his mouth lifted in that half smile that had a way of melting her. "You can check my references. I've never hit anyone. I may startle, but I've never thrown a punch."

She slid into the chair next to him as he lifted his sandwich. "Speaking of references, Ryan called. Tushar and Trish are back in the bunker. He texted me their numbers if you want to call them. Ryan says he'll bring them here when he brings us supplies."

"Oh, good. Yeah, I have some questions. Mostly for Ryan, but his parents might be able to answer some of them too. I don't know how ingrained they've gotten in the various studies yet. They probably aren't too up-to-date since they've been hiding away from the bunker too."

She gave a shrug. "Depends on if they're as dedicated to their work as you are. I mean, it would stand to reason that since all of you were working long hours for little thanks for months and even years before you were infected and then preserved, most of you might pick up where you left off. All four of you have indicated you felt like you had woken up from a nap rather than a ten-year vitrification."

"Yeah, that part's true. It was strange to find out how much time had gone by. But I'm not sure everyone who wakes up will have the urge to jump back into medicine. Emily seems slightly hesitant, though I'm pretty sure that's because she feels so far behind on the developments in the lab. Which I can totally relate to."

Blair nodded. "Yeah. She and I have become good friends. You're right about her. She is dedicated, though. She's taking classes and doing her part at the same time. I can tell you that Tushar buried himself in the lab the moment he could stand. Trish, on the other hand, was yanked out of the bunker after three weeks. She was pissed."

"I can imagine. After all, she probably wanted to spend time with Ryan. I'm not a woman, but I think I can at least acknowledge women have a bond with their kids no one else can compete with."

Blair picked up her sandwich to take another bite. "Perhaps." She couldn't relate, not just because she wasn't a mother, but also because her own mother had not had that kind of bond with either Blair or her sister.

Not before Jen died and not after.

"You okay?"

She lifted her gaze, realizing she was picking on the corner of her sandwich, deep in thought. "Yes. Of course." She sat up straighter.

He lifted his brow again. "Uh-huh. You think fathers can bond just as well with their kids?"

"Sometimes…" Why were they having this discussion?

"Did yours?"

Well, fuck. She stood and carried her plate to the sink, dumping the remains of her sandwich in the trash. She had no idea how this conversation had gotten so far off track. When she returned, noticing his plate was empty also, she reached for it.

But Dade stopped her by grabbing her hand and giving it a tug to get her attention. "I hit a nerve."

She sucked in a breath, staring at their connection. His thumb was stroking the back of her hand. "No. Don't worry. It's fine."

"It's not fine. You haven't told me about your parents. You only mentioned that you had a sister who passed away. I'm so sorry about that. And, it's okay if you don't want to talk about it. I just wanted you to know I was paying attention. Then and now."

She nodded, fighting back emotion, still not meeting his gaze. Damn him for being so nice after she'd spent every waking hour convincing herself of all the reasons she needed to keep her distance from him.

"I may seem preoccupied most of the time, and while that is true, I'm not an ass when it matters. Slap me upside the head when you need my attention. I swear I will not bite."

She nodded again, pulled her hand free, and turned back to the sink with his plate. With her back to him, she shook off thoughts of the past and forced herself back to the present. "I was thinking I could help you."

"Help me how? You are helping me. You've gone above and beyond what any human being could be expected to do to keep me safe. And you made this commitment without knowing a thing about me. Someone else could have volunteered to protect me, but they didn't. You did."

She blushed, facing him again as she leaned against the counter. "It's my job."

He stood and sauntered closer to her while he spoke. "It's more than a job. It's an enormous commitment. I realize we're way up in the mountains in a remote cabin, and most of the time it seems like we're just two people hanging out. But you know as well as I do that all three people who were reanimated before me have faced attack."

She sucked in a sharp breath when he stopped moving, inches from her.

"It's only a matter of time before my name gets out there, and then who knows what will happen. I've read through the notes about what happened to Emily and then Tushar and Trish. They thought they were safe. They were wrong." He reached for her, one finger touching just under her chin, captivating her with that simple touch.

"You're safe," she managed to whisper.

His brows were drawn together. Serious. He held her gaze with those deep chocolate eyes that would melt any woman. "My name will get out, and then the hunt will begin. If there's a mole, I'll be a target too."

"This time only a few people know where you are, and very few more know of your existence."

He nodded slowly. "I'm racing against two clocks. One ticks for the treatment to cure this damn mutation of anemia. The other ticks for the continued secrecy of my existence. Both clocks will run out."

She grabbed his biceps with both hands, pain stabbing at her chest. "They don't have to."

"They will," he insisted. "And that's okay. I'm aware of the danger I'm in on both fronts."

She swallowed, tears forming in her eyes. She never cried. Never. Not since Jen died and her heart froze in her chest. "I'll protect you."

He leaned closer.

She squeezed his arms, gulping back the emotion. Stopping it. Knowing that it still showed on her face. Unable to protect herself from him. Unable to protect herself from the passage of time.

"I need to know something."

"What?"

His lips were inches from hers. He slowly closed that distance, his eyes holding her hostage.

The moment his lips touched hers, she lost her breath.

His touch was hesitant at first, and then he tilted his head to one side to deepen the kiss.

She opened for him instantly, her heart racing. She rose onto her tiptoes to bring herself closer to him, grasping his arms tighter.

The finger under her chin trailed around to her neck and then up to her ear.

And then, just as suddenly as he'd started this kiss, he ended it, pulling back, still holding her gaze.

His next words couldn't have stunned her more. "You have to go back to the bunker. I need to take off on my own."

CHAPTER 9

"What?" She was still dazed from the best kiss she'd ever experienced, thinking she must have misheard him. As she lowered her heels to the floor, she searched his face.

He smirked. "You're into me."

She flushed deeper. He was so cocky. Instead of responding, she furrowed her brow.

He shrugged. "We can't continue this."

"Continue what?" Sweat beaded on her forehead even though it was not hot in the cabin.

"This arrangement. I can't be with you."

"Why the hell not?" She was getting a little pissed, half with him and half with herself. She didn't want to start something with him either for dozens of reasons, but it still stung to have him blatantly point out he was uninterested. And why was he being so arrogant?

"Because I want to fuck you. It's distracting."

She released his arms and set her hands on her hips. Was he trying to be a dick? "Okay. I'm not sure why you have to be so crude about it. And I'm sorry you find me so distracting. But my job is to protect you. Surely you can keep your dick in your pants while I do my job." She had no idea why she chose to respond to his crude language with her own.

He ran a hand through his hair and stepped back. "Don't take it personal, but this isn't a good fit. I don't need a bodyguard anyway. I can fire a weapon. I'll be fine."

"What the hell are you talking about? This isn't up to you." He was all over the place. One kiss and he seemed to have lost a few marbles. Or the entire jar.

"I'm pretty certain I still have free will. I can decline assistance if I want. And I'm exercising that right. You need to go back to the bunker."

She lifted both brows. "Not a chance in hell. I have no idea what's going on inside that head of yours, but you need to snap out of it. You're stuck here with me for the duration." At the moment, half of her wanted to give him his wish and walk right out the front door. Lucky for him, the ground was covered with a foot of snow, making it impossible for her to leave.

He shook his head. Defiant.

"What the hell, Dade?" She shoved off the counter and rushed toward him, slamming her hands against his chest in frustration.

He grabbed her wrists, shocking her with his ability to restrain her. She wouldn't have thought he would have the energy yet. "You can't stay with me."

"Why? Give me one goddamn good reason why?" she shouted, tugging on her wrists.

"Because I care about you," he retorted, also shouting. "Because you're kind and funny and cute and strong and you kiss like an angel...and you're into me."

She jerked her head back, still pressing against his chest with her fists. "That makes no sense. Why would you want me to leave if you think I'm so amazing?"

"Because I can't risk anything happening to you while you protect me. It would kill me. And I won't have you watching me die. I'd rather end it now than see the look in your eyes as I get sick and then slowly die."

"Don't you dare even fucking suggest such a thing." She was shaking, her entire body on alert, a chill and a sweat breaking out at the same time. She shook her head. "Never. Don't ever fucking joke about taking your life. *Ever.* You hear me? It's not fucking funny."

He stiffened, frowning. "Jesus, Blair. It was a figure of speech. I wasn't talking about suicide. I'm talking about us. We have to end this relationship before it begins. I won't do this to you."

Now she was fuming. "Do *what* to me? I think you're trying to escape having to *feel.* Feel anything at all. You think it'll be easier for you if you crawl into a cave alone to die so that it won't hurt so bad? Don't put this on me. It's you who doesn't want to receive kindness from someone because you're worried about hurting yourself.

"One ill-timed kiss and you think you get to change the game and run away." She shook her head. "Not a chance in hell. I signed on to this job because you need me. You *still* need me. And I'm damn well going to keep you alive. For much longer than you seem to believe."

"That's crazy. You've been reading too many psychology books. Don't try to climb into my head and tell me how to feel. I'm perfectly fine. Thank you for shaking me up when I most needed it. I'm standing on my own two feet now. I can walk alone. Go back to the bunker and find someone else to rescue."

She was struggling to keep from crying, drained from thinking he had suggested that he might kill himself. She needed to get away from him. She need air. She needed to lie down before she passed out. She jerked her hands free and jumped back to put distance between them. "It's not going to happen, so get over yourself, and ditch that cocky attitude super fast, because you're stuck here with me whether you like it or not.

"I'm a grown woman, perfectly capable of deciding what I'm

willing to do. You don't get to make choices for me. I was paid to do this job, and I'm not leaving." She crossed her arms defiantly. "If kissing me is that big of a distraction to you, then don't fucking do it again. But I'm here until the bitter end, whatever that might look like."

She had no idea why she was arguing her point so fiercely when what she should be doing was agreeing with him, getting the hell out of Dodge, and letting him go it alone. It would be a safer route as far as her own heart was concerned. But for some reason, she couldn't stand the idea of him thinking he could make demands of her and she would simply defer to him and walk out the door.

Or maybe she was kidding herself, and she should admit that kiss meant something and accept she had feelings for him. Her hard and fast personal rule to never let her heart get entangled with anyone was teetering on the edge of disaster.

She narrowed her gaze, hands on her hips, fighting the urge to walk away, forcing herself to be the bigger person. "You have two choices—keep your distance or take me up on my offer to help with your research. I might not know anything about science, but I can follow directions."

"Help me?" He flinched.

"Yeah, help you. You know, when one person offers their time in exchange for nothing. A volunteer? Ring a bell?"

He stared at her like she had two heads. "That's a terrible idea."

She fumed, unsure if he was insinuating she was too stupid to be of assistance or that he didn't want her so close to him. Either way, she was tapped out of emotional control. This conversation was officially over. "Fuck you," she shouted out of self-preservation, as she stomped from the kitchen, slammed the door to her bedroom, and turned the lock.

～

Dade stood in the kitchen, staring at her bedroom door, the first door in the hallway. He could still hear the banging sound of it slamming as if it were on an infinite echo. He could also hear her last words ringing in his head. *Fuck you.*

He had no idea what came over him. Why did he kiss her in the first place? She'd been standing so close and smelled so good, and she wore another one of those damn tight shirts that accentuated her chest and the fucking leggings that showed off every muscle in her legs and ass. Her eyes. The blue was like a siren's call.

He had no idea what to do either. She had thrown him completely off balance with her comebacks. He'd meant for this to be simple. He told her to leave, and she left. He should have known it wouldn't go down like that, but he hadn't been thinking clearly. The moment his lips touched hers, he knew he needed to end this thing before it started, so he blurted the first thing that came to mind.

If he wasn't so flummoxed at the moment, he would laugh at the absurdity of thinking he could simply order her to leave and expect her to walk away. She wasn't that kind of woman. She was strong and powerful and bossy. The same qualities he found attractive.

She had also told him where he could stuff his plan.

He was in way over his head now. He never should have crossed that line with her. *Fuck.* Not only had he kissed her, but he'd been a huge asshole afterward. Unnecessarily crude. Telling a woman you wanted to fuck her was probably not the best line. He'd made it sound like she was a hot piece of ass instead of a human being with feelings.

He started pacing in order to clear his head. When that didn't help, he stopped to stare out the back door at the snow. The sun was bright, but it was too cold for the snow to melt. Even the icicles hanging off the roof were there to stay, much like the owner of the cabin.

He had fucked things up good. He should go talk to her.

On second thought, she hadn't seemed receptive to that idea as she left the room.

There was no way in hell he could let himself get involved with her or even feel anything for her. It would cloud his mind and distract him from what he really needed to be doing. Research. His exploration had grown beyond tinkering with the treatment that hadn't been perfected.

This morning he'd had a new idea. Surely someone somewhere in the world had survived this new mutation of AA2. He needed to find them. He needed more hours in the day.

He needed an assistant.

He spun around and stared at her bedroom door again. "Fuck." That had been exactly what Blair had been suggesting when he'd lost his mind and touched her lips with his.

Leaning against the door, he pondered this new development further. He could continue to demand she leave, but he felt certain no matter how much he argued with her, he would lose. She was determined.

He sure as hell couldn't kiss her again. Or even touch her. He needed her to wear more clothes too. If she insisted on putting her life in danger for him, he would have to figure out a way to live through it.

He wasn't a complete asshole, for heaven's sake. He could keep his dick in his pants. She was just a cute woman. The world was filled with women. None of them had managed to derail him from life before. This one wouldn't either.

Right.

Now he just needed to talk to her. Probably later would be better. She was pissed when she left him standing there. Instead, he decided to use his time coming up with a plan that would delegate some of his workload to his new assistant. They would need another computer. Ryan could bring one when he came with supplies. In the meantime, he could print out the data from the bunker's research and work with that while she used the computer.

After a lot of thinking and planning and talking himself down from the ledge, he started making dinner. A peace offering. Perhaps the scents would lure her out of her room without him having to go get her.

As soon as he had the pasta sauce simmering, she opened the door and leaned against the frame, arms crossed, face hard. "Is this how you expect to convince me to leave? With Italian food? It's your worst skill set?"

He chuckled, crossing the room toward her. "No. It's how I intend to apologize."

She took a deep breath, her eyes fluttering. "It might work."

"I'm sorry," he said when he reached her. "I was a dick. I shouldn't have overreacted, and I shouldn't have kissed you. It was insensitive and rude. I didn't even ask. I just took without warning. It was also unprofessional, and for all intents and purposes, we're like coworkers."

She stared at him, mouth dropping open.

He didn't give her a chance to speak, however. "It won't happen again. I promise. And if you're still willing, I would love for you to help me research."

She rolled her eyes. "You didn't exactly force me to kiss you, Dade. I was a willing participant. I should have backed away, but I didn't. I wanted to know as badly as you did. And now we know." Her gaze was direct, unfaltering.

He read between the lines at her meaning. Yeah, now they knew. But they would just have to ignore that revelation and stuff it into a closet.

"I'm sorry too," she continued. "It was unprofessional for me as well. It can't happen again. I can't do my job if I'm constantly distracted by…other things."

"Speaking of distracted…" he glanced at her chest and then back up, "…don't you have any big sweatshirts or something you could wear?" He waved a hand through the air in the general direction of her body. She was still wearing the fitted shirt from earlier and those damn skintight pants.

She hugged her arms tighter under her chest, making it rise, while she narrowed her gaze and gave him the evil eye. "You're kidding, right?"

"No," he murmured.

"Well, get over yourself. This is who I am. It's how I'm comfortable. Are you going to keep working out with nothing but shorts on?" She lifted a brow.

He smirked. "Are you going to keep working out wearing less material than what makes up my shorts?" he retorted.

"Are you saying you can't control yourself in front of me?" Now she had a full smile. "Interesting."

"Why is that interesting?" His hands were shaking, and he fisted them at his sides. "You're thirty-five years old. Don't tell me you aren't aware of your appeal. I don't believe for a second that men don't come on to you every day." It occurred to him that maybe someone had who shouldn't have. Perhaps her commanding officer had done more than she'd let on, which would shed further light on her decision to leave the army.

"This is the twenty-first century. I work in a man's world. Every one of my coworkers knows better than to treat me with any less respect than they would anyone else in the room. If they did, they would be in hot water. You should know that. You were in the military yourself. Did you have trouble keeping your dick in your pants when you were enlisted?"

Oh, she was on fire. He needed to keep his wits to spar with her. "Of course not."

"Then how is this different?"

"We aren't in the barracks. We're in a small cabin. Alone."

She rolled her eyes again. "Fine. You start wearing a sweatshirt and sweatpants when you work out."

"That's crazy. I'd burn up."

She lifted both brows. "So it's okay for you to expose your entire chest, but I can't have just my abs showing? If you want to be equal, I could stop wearing a bra."

He groaned. "Not the same thing."

"Of course it is. Your chest is smoking hot. I don't know how you managed to keep so toned for ten years. It's crazy. It's a wonder I don't drop a weight on my foot when you flex."

He flinched, shocked at her admission.

"Look, the truth is, we're physically attracted to each other. It happens. Doesn't mean we can't ignore it. We're adults. We might even be irrationally lustful because there's no one else around. So...we agree to ignore it and get back to work. We have a disease to cure. We don't have time for distractions."

He searched her face. She was serious. No way was he going to point out that he didn't think it would work when she obviously was convinced they could pretend that kiss never happened.

If she truly believed any of that horseshit, then she wasn't half as into him as he was her. But she was right. He needed to rein in the little head and ignore its demands. He nodded. "You're right."

"Now, feed me. That sauce smells delicious." She flattened a palm on his chest as she walked past him, making his heart flutter.

As he watched her firm ass move into the kitchen, he groaned silently. She was going to be a challenge. Lucky for him, he never shied away from a challenge.

CHAPTER 10

One week later...

Dade opened the front door as Ryan pulled up to the cabin. He'd never been so relieved to see other humans in his life.

To say the last week had been challenging would be an understatement. He and Blair had settled into a routine that worked for them. He usually hit the home gym before her in the mornings so they didn't have to share the space more than necessary. Then she worked out while he cooked breakfast.

After that, he spent the mornings on the computer while she cleaned the kitchen and then retreated to her room for a while to shower and give him space. After lunch, she worked on the computer, looking up whatever he suggested while he went through notes. Sometimes he used her iPad.

Their routine was about to change now that Ryan was bringing them another computer.

When Tushar and Trish stepped out of the same delivery truck that had transported Dade and Blair the week before, Dade's smile widened. He rushed down the porch stairs to greet them. Without a word, he gave Tushar a giant hug and then Trish. "Damn," he said, as he held her at arm's length. "It's like not a day went by."

She smiled. "For you too. It's so weird."

Blair brushed by Dade to greet their guests too. "Welcome. Come on inside. It's freezing out here."

Everyone grabbed several bags from the back of the truck and then headed for the cabin.

Dade put the groceries away while the rest of them took seats at the table. After all, he was the one who made the list, and he would be the one doing most of the cooking.

Everyone talked over one another, sharing news and events and life. When Dade finally slid onto a stool at the end of the table between Ryan and Tushar, he found both men looking at him.

Tushar cleared his throat. "A strange thing happened. I didn't want to say anything until I was sure it was legitimate."

Dade's heart stopped, thinking they had found a possible cure, which would have been absurd if he paused to think about it. He was as privy to the data as anyone else, and it wasn't rational. He took a breath when he realized this mysterious topic had to be unrelated.

"So, you know that your grandfather passed away three years ago?"

"Yes."

"Well, he left you his estate."

"Pardon?" Dade jerked back a few inches. "How is that even possible? He had no idea I would ever be reanimated. Could he even do that?"

Tushar nodded.

Ryan spoke next. "I looked into it. A person can do anything they want with their money, no matter how absurd it might seem, as long as they have someone to follow their wishes. Your grandfather assigned an executor to the estate. Apparently he saved a lot of money in his old age. He never needed nursing care, and he died peacefully in his sleep. He kept stashing money away, just in case."

"How do you know all this?" Dade was still confused.

"I met with the executor yesterday. He didn't tell me how much money was in the estate, but he was free with the rest of the information. He had no choice. I was extremely skeptical about his validity."

"We all were," Trish added. "I'm still leery."

"Wait. How does he know about me?"

"He doesn't," Tushar added. "He only knows that some people have been reanimated. So, he contacted Temple a few months ago when he heard the news."

"This is crazy." Dade leaned back in his chair. "Are you sure he's not just some asshole fishing for information?"

Ryan nodded. "Temple checked him out thoroughly a while back. He even has a letter your grandfather left for her and another one for you. Your grandfather explained to Temple that you had given him her contact information even before you got sick, just in case anything would ever happen to you or he couldn't reach you for some reason."

Dade nodded. That was true.

Ryan continued, "Your grandfather must have been a bit eccentric. Or at least an optimist. He left instructions for the executor to hold his estate for you for fifty years, at which time he wanted the money to be donated to cryonics research. If you weren't reanimated within fifty years, he thought the funds should at least go toward continued research that would give you a chance."

Dade was stunned. "I never knew my grandfather to have any money at all. I'd be surprised if it was anything substantial."

"Well, the executor acts like it is," Ryan added.

"Don't forget," Tushar said, "you had some money too.

Everything you owned went to your grandfather when you were preserved."

"Huh. This is so insane."

"Granted, we have one little problem," Tushar pointed out. "We don't want the executor to know you're alive just yet. It's too risky. As far as he knows, he's done his job by informing Temple the money exists. Ryan assured him that when and if you were reanimated, you would be informed."

"Right. Makes sense. But I can't very well enjoy my inheritance if I don't collect it."

"We're trying to figure something out," Trish said. "I've been working with Temple. We'll have to arrange for some sort of non-disclosure agreement for the executor. But even more difficult is going to be arranging for him to meet with you. You have to be present to sign the documents and receive them. The guy can't just take our word for it and hand over your inheritance."

"Of course." That was a problem. "And I'm contagious." It was hard to remember that Dade needed to keep his distance from the general population.

"Exactly." Ryan sighed. "But we'll figure something out."

As the conversation turned to a discussion about the protesters and how Trish and Tushar were familiarizing themselves with the most up-to-date medical research, Dade kept thinking about that inheritance and what it could mean to him.

If he had that money, he could potentially get the cure for AP12 and then leave the state if he wanted. He could travel for his remaining days. He wouldn't have to continue to be a burden on the government or Blair, in particular.

His chest squeezed at the thought of not seeing her anymore, but it would be so much easier if he could cut ties with her entirely. *Easier for you? Or for her?*

When there was a lull in the conversation, Dade set his elbows on the table and brought up the subject he'd been waiting to discuss. "Talk to me about autologous stem cell transplantation."

His question was directed to the room at large, with the exception of Blair. But she looked curious too. Maybe she had seen the term in their research.

Ryan nodded slowly. "It's a possibility. As a last resort. There's no data to suggest it would work. You're one of a kind."

"I get that, but you're surely considering that angle, and right now you don't have a magic cure, and I'm not on a bone marrow transplant registry. Using my own stem cells just makes sense."

Tushar agreed. "I've been working that angle extensively, actually." He set a hand on Dade's shoulder. "Not ruling it out."

"In the end, it's kinda my best choice, right? It's the easiest solution. Far less invasive than a bone marrow transplant, and it might work. At the very least, it would allow me to leave this cabin, travel, and enjoy myself for as long as it lasts." This idea seemed far more appealing now that he knew there was at least some sort of nest egg he could use to travel.

Trish winced. "There's no data," she reminded everyone.

"But it might work," Tushar conceded. "Let's give it some more time to percolate. I've already organized a team to try something similar in the lab."

"On rats?" Dade asked. Studies on lab rats were always a toss-up when it came to human application.

"Yes. Do you have a better idea?" Tushar removed his hand from Dade's shoulder.

"Yes. Me." Dade sat up straighter.

Trish gave a sharp inhale. "You've shown no signs of AP12 yet. Let's not invent problems. We have time."

Not a lot of it.

The moment the delivery truck pulled away and Blair stepped back inside behind Dade, she pounced. "Tell me what all that transplant talk was about. I didn't want to interrupt the greatest scientific minds of the universe bumping into each other, but give it to me in layman's terms now."

He slumped down on the couch and leaned back.

Instead of sitting in the armchair she usually occupied, she sat next to him. "Please. Talk to me."

"Okay," he told the ceiling. "So, before I was preserved, they removed my blood."

"Right. I think I knew that. They replaced it with some sort of cryoprotectant to keep the tissues from being damaged from ice formation."

He lowered his gaze to smile. "You're an expert."

"Hardly. Keep going."

"The team removed my stem cells from the blood and saved them. They were also frozen, so to speak."

She nodded. "Got it. People sometimes save their baby's stem cells."

"Exactly. Nowadays, adults can even have their blood separated and the stem cells removed. Not exactly the same, but close."

"I see."

He twisted his body to more fully face her. "Theoretically, those cells are clean. In fact they're actually very clean because I don't have any symptoms of AA2. If I was in the full-blown stages of AA2 before the cells were removed, they would be contaminated. Since they're not, it's possible that I could be given the treatment for AP12 and immediately receive a transfusion of my own stem cells which could—again in theory—force my bone marrow to do what it's supposed to do and never allow AA2 to form."

"Why doesn't anyone think it will work?"

"It's never been done in this scenario before. There's no way to know. No one except Trish, Tushar, and Emily have ever had their blood totally drained and replaced ten years later. No one has had that first batch of stem cells from a total blood removal saved for future use. It's a crap shoot."

"But you feel confident?" She sat up straighter.

"Not particularly. But it's better than nothing."

"And we have time."

"We do. But the treatment stands a much greater chance of working if I'm not sick when they do it. So, waiting until I have symptoms of AP12 is a bad idea also."

"What do you want to do?"

"I don't know yet. I don't want to think about it at all right now." He rubbed his arm where Ryan had taken a blood sample before he left.

She was certain it didn't hurt, but the small puncture was a reminder that they would be waiting for Ryan to run some tests and ensure Dade still had no active signs of AP12.

Anemia and its various mutations were starting to infiltrate her nightmares.

She decided to change the subject to something she hoped would be more uplifting. "Four more people will be awake next week, right?" Originally the team only had one reanimation chamber, but after two successful revivals—Emily and Tushar—three more chambers were ordered. Now four people were due to come out of a coma in a few days.

"Yes." He smiled. "And all of them are free of AA2, so they won't be facing what I am."

"That's great. Were you close to any of them?"

"I'm close to all of the members of my team. There were twenty-one of us in total, and we were working night and day in close quarters for months before we succumbed to AP12 and had to be preserved. However, my closest friend was Zeke Holleran. I'm looking forward to seeing him."

"It must be weird. I mean, it's been years, but it's also been days."

"Yes. That part is strange. I just saw Tushar and Trish and Emily a few weeks ago in my mind. Zeke too."

"What's he like?" Blair was enjoying this easy camaraderie. Calmly sitting together on the couch. Talking. The frantic pace Dade usually set each day was on the back burner for now. He seemed content to absorb everything he'd learned in the last few hours instead of rushing back to work.

"Zeke?" Dade rolled his head back and forth across the couch cushion. He undoubtedly had kinks in his neck. "He's hard-working, serious, incredibly smart. He has a PhD in Immunology. Good guy. I hope he comes out of this unscathed."

"Was anyone on the team married? I mean, besides Tushar and Trish." There were nineteen other people. Surely they weren't all single. What would have happened to their spouses?

But Dade shook his head. "Believe it or not, no. The only other person who was ever married was Zeke, actually. He married a nursing student he met at Harvard where he got his PhD after the Naval Academy. She married him for money, however, thinking he was going to be a wealthy guy. Little did she know, he had no interest in money at all, and even less interest in possessions."

"Bet that didn't go over well."

Dade chuckled. "Not at all. When he took this job with Project DEEP, she was not happy. She hated living in an apartment in Falling Rock, Colorado, so she left him."

Blair cringed. "Ouch."

"It was for the best. I didn't know him before he arrived, but I think she did a number on him. He never dated anyone the entire time we worked together."

"What about you?" she asked.

He shot her a glance, that devastating half smile making her wish she hadn't asked. "Me? Did I date?"

"Yeah." Reasonable enough question.

"Some. Not often. This job is not super conducive to extracurricular activities. I had an apartment in town, but I rarely went there in the last six months or so before I was preserved. And even when I did go home to sleep in my own bed, I didn't know enough people in town to date if I wanted to. Usually, I just wanted to sleep."

"That sounds kinda depressing." She didn't mean to insult him, but she couldn't imagine him so cut off from society that he had no social life.

He shrugged. "I guess. Honestly, I didn't think much about it. I was dedicated to my job. We all were. It comes with the territory. No one took a job with Project DEEP without about a dozen layers of interviews and extreme vetting. It was a highly coveted position. Most of the team was under thirty and single with a one-track mind. Curing diseases."

"So you were the old guy. A whopping thirty-five," she joked.

"Except for Tushar and Trish. And they even had a kid." He sat up straighter and twisted toward her again. "Talk about weird. Waking up to find their son, Ryan Anand, in charge of the new team was the strangest thing ever. I remember that kid as a teenager. Of course, I'm not surprised. He had science and medicine in his genes. Plus, he had motivation—saving his own parents."

Blair leaned the side of her head against the couch, smiling. This was nice. Easy. Comfortable. They weren't touching each other, but they were facing and very close. In a different world, she would climb on top of this man and force him to see her as more than a coworker.

Actually, she knew he did see her as more, but it would be wonderful if he could or would act on it.

What the hell was she thinking? At no point in her life had she wished for such a thing with any man, but somehow everything was different with Dade.

He surprised her with his next question. "What about you? Do you date much?"

She gave him a wry smile. "Not often. Not in a long time."

"Why?" His brow was furrowed in serious confusion.

She shrugged. "I never seem to click with anyone, I guess. When I have the opportunity to meet men I don't already know, they usually back away from me pretty quickly." She immediately felt like she'd said too much. At the same time she had not said enough.

"What?" His voice rose. "That's crazy. Why would anyone back away from you?"

She laughed. "Really? You have to ask?"

He lifted his head and stared her down so hard she shivered. "Yes. I'm lost. You're gorgeous. Sexy. Funny. Hard-working. The list goes on. Why would anyone in their right mind not be in line for a turn to date you?"

A flush rushed over her cheeks. That's what he thought of her? "Dade, most men take a step back when they find out I was in the military and work as a bodyguard. And to their credit, I can be overbearing and dominating." She realized she hadn't said that quite right and wound her fingers together, fidgeting.

He pasted on a fake look of shock, placing a palm over his heart. "You? Overbearing and dominating?"

She swallowed, almost hurt at his attitude. She knew he didn't mean anything by it, but he didn't quite get what she was trying to say. She needed to put an end to this. The feel-good moment had passed.

Setting her palms on her knees, she exhaled and gave him one more parting thought. "I hear you. You're not wrong. I can be bossy by nature and by profession. If I wasn't domineering in my job, people would get killed. But here's the thing—people have a tendency to assume those characteristics extend to every aspect of my life. Men take a step back, afraid to tangle with someone who they fear will top them at all times. My job is my job. It doesn't define who I am outside of work."

Dade nodded slowly.

She suddenly felt like she'd divulged too much. Gotten too

personal. She had no interest in expounding on anything she'd just said. When he opened his mouth to respond, she stood and rushed from the room to the only part of the house where she had privacy.

Shutting the door to her bedroom, she leaned against it and slid down to the floor. She leaned her head against her knees and cringed. How did their pleasant afternoon turn into something so personal?

CHAPTER 11

Dade didn't move for a long time. He stared at her closed bedroom door, not even blinking. A tornado had just rushed through the room and left him disheveled and out of breath.

When he finally blinked and leaned back, her words were still swimming around in his head, needing to be dissected.

Men take a step back, afraid to tangle with someone who they fear will top them at all times.

My job is my job. It doesn't define who I am outside of work.

He ran a hand through his hair. *Fuck me.*

He'd give anything to have a lengthy explanation about what she meant by that little monologue. So many thoughts went through his mind. A jumbled disjointed mess.

He inhaled long and slow, trying to make sense out of her words. It seemed like she was saying that she wasn't always bossy. Did she mean in the bedroom? He swallowed, trying not to let his mind wander to the possibilities.

He couldn't imagine why anyone would be intimidated by her personality to begin with. Yes, she was pushy, but it didn't bother him at all. He would never judge a woman by her tendency to dominate. He was secure enough to go toe-to-toe with just about anyone. Inside or outside the bedroom.

It was actually refreshing to find someone who could hold up their end of the conversation and keep him interested. Not *all* men needed to feel superior to their partners. He found her ability to communicate far more appealing.

It didn't even bother him that she knew very little about his profession. She was educated, curious, and interested in his work. And she gave him her full attention when he spoke about things most women would find incredibly boring. If he met a woman who was excited about her work and outgoing enough to speak her mind, and it spilled over into the bedroom, he didn't mind one way or the other.

If Blair thought it was hard to find men who didn't mind her job as a personal security detail, she should try finding women who could tolerate an extremely intelligent biomedical scientist. Talk about intimidating.

Dating was always a balancing act. He wanted to say enough about himself to ensure the woman knew who he really was, but not so much that she was intimidated, turned off, or bored. He could often judge by a woman's eyes and body language where the night was going within minutes of meeting her.

He winced when he realized the similarities between him and Blair. Both of them were in a constant battle not to be judged by their cover. Her book cover was badass female, military drill sergeant. His book cover was nerdy science guy. He had also been in the military, but that wasn't what stood out when people met him. He'd never been in combat or even overseas.

The point was that they both faced stereotypes that created difficult hurdles. Often it simply wasn't worth it to attempt to prove to his dates otherwise. If they couldn't give him a chance because they prejudged him, then he didn't want to expend the energy to set them straight.

Did Blair feel the same way? Maybe that was why she didn't

date. He certainly wouldn't want to put effort into showing someone he could be less dominant in other situations.

He closed his eyes and took another deep breath. Picturing Blair as submissive in the bedroom had his blood pumping. Not so much because he felt the need to top a woman when he had sex, but more because he couldn't stop visualizing Blair in bed, period. Top. Bottom. Hovering over him. Pinned under him. Damn. He didn't care. He just wanted her there.

Most of every day he suppressed those types of thoughts. He'd done so successfully for over a week. But it was difficult. The more he knew her, the more he liked her. A lot. He could ignore that fact, but it wouldn't go away.

She was all those things he'd said and more. Kind. Funny. Warm. Cheerful. Upbeat. Smart. Strong.

She couldn't cook. There. A flaw. An endearing one, however. Cute.

Dammit. There was no easy way to get through this craziness. What if he approached her again sexually?

He winced at the thought that she would probably shoot him down. He could be persuasive when he needed to be, but the idea of talking a woman into sleeping with him held no appeal.

He could flirt with her a bit more to see if she took the bait and returned the gesture, but that was a cop out. He didn't habitually resort to such cheap measures to get a woman to look at him.

What are you thinking?

Shaking such preposterous thoughts from his head, he headed for the back door. It was nice out. Cold but sunny and not snowing. The perfect day to swing that axe of hers, blow off some stress, and add to her pile.

Ironic?

Probably. After all that thinking about how he didn't need to belittle Blair to make himself feel superior, the last thing he should do was remind her of one of their earliest confrontations.

But the exercise and fresh air would do him good, and besides, this challenge had been set in motion over a week ago. He couldn't back down now. Time to prove he was catching up to her physically.

~

Blair couldn't help but smile and even laugh out loud as she lay on her bed, staring at the ceiling, listening to that axe coming down over and over. She wasn't sure what his message was or even if he had one, but she couldn't find the will to be offended.

She had left him with confusing words that part of her would prefer to take back. For a long time, the cabin had remained silent while she lay on her bed, and he undoubtedly pondered her statements.

When she heard the back door close, she wondered what he was up to. She didn't like the idea of him outside alone. After all, it was her job to keep him safe. On the flip side, nothing would emasculate him more than for her to berate him for stepping out back. It was a fine line.

The first time the axe hit the log, she nearly jumped out of her skin before realizing what the sound was. Heart racing, she lowered onto her back and listened to the soothing rhythmic sound of the hatchet.

If he was making a statement, she heard it. He was stronger now. He no longer felt like he wasn't her equal. She found it hard to believe the Dade she knew would go to this length to intentionally make her feel weak or less capable than him. Especially not after the words she'd last spoken.

Dade was always courteous. He was thoughtful enough to take her statements seriously.

Or maybe he just wanted to get outside and hit something to blow off steam. She smiled again. Also possible.

The man had stamina. That was for sure. He kept at it.

An idea popped into her mind. If he could chop her wood, she could cook in his kitchen. Right?

Might not have been her best idea, but it seemed like an unspoken truce. Equalizing them. Putting them back to rights after her admission that she wasn't always in the mood to be the master of the world.

As she headed for the kitchen, she watched him out the window. He had taken off his coat and was methodically working through the logs she had piled up several yards from the house. Every time he lifted the hatchet, she sucked in a breath. He was an Adonis. His back was sculpted and mouthwatering. His biceps and forearms had gotten firmer. Even his ass inside his formfitting jeans was delectable.

Unable to resist his magnetic pull, she made the spontaneous decision to join him outside. She tugged on her boots and grabbed her coat from the hook before opening the back door.

They spent so much time in such a serious mood. They needed a diversion.

Dade swung the axe at the same moment she shut the door, so he didn't notice her approaching, which gave her a devious idea. She bent down, picked up a pile of snow, molded it into a ball, and launched it at his back as soon as he set the axe down to grab another log.

She hit her target dead on, making him spin around. His eyes were wide with confusion. She smirked as she grabbed another handful of snow and took aim again, this time hitting him in the chest before he had a chance to respond.

Thank God he smiled and dropped the log. Seconds later, he had his own snowball and nailed her in the thigh.

"What kind of aim is that?" she taunted.

"Really?" he asked. "You want to go there?"

She launched another packed ball at him, hitting him in the cheek this time.

His face was red, but his eyes sparkled with mirth. It was a much better look than the usual serious expression he held. "Blair..." he warned. He grabbed another handful of snow and came toward her.

She jumped back and then ran around the edge of the cabin. The moment he rounded behind her into her line of sight, only feet separating them, she landed another crudely constructed snowball against his belly.

He had two in his hands, however, and he recovered quickly, throwing both in rapid succession, hitting her in the upper arm and then the back of the head as she ducked.

She bent down to compile more snow, but he rushed forward, tagged her around the waist, and smashed a handful of snow into her face from behind.

She sputtered and gasped. It was freezing cold. "Hey, you don't play fair."

"Is there a rule book for sneaking up behind someone and starting a snowball fight without their knowledge?" he joked as he rubbed more snow into her cheek. He still held her firmly against him, her back to his front. With only one free hand, he had her pinned and managed to do sufficient damage with the icy cold fluff.

She grabbed his forearm, trying to free herself. "Yes. Of course there are rules. Haven't you ever been in a snowball fight before?"

His lips were close to her ear when he responded. "It's been a while. I didn't realize it wasn't a contact sport."

She giggled, taking advantage of his momentary distraction, and wiggled free by dropping her weight to duck under his arm and scramble away. As she stumbled, she reached out with her hands to catch herself.

Dade was on her in an instant, hauling her back up to standing while he scooped another pile of snow to smash into her neck this time.

She hadn't zipped her coat up all the way, so the cold wetness ran down inside her shirt, making her squeal. "Uncle," she shouted.

Finally, he released her. "That's what I thought."

She attempted to brush the freezing snow off her chest, only making it worse. Shivering, she met his gaze. "Cheater."

He was grinning wide as he shrugged. "You shouldn't sneak up on a man with an axe."

"I waited until you set it down."

"Ah. Well, then. That makes all the difference." His cheeks were pink. He'd never looked more alive. It was a good look on him. At least she'd made him forget his problems for a few minutes.

Her instinct was to close the distance, tip her head back, and kiss him again. She wasn't sure how he would respond, though, so instead, she decided it was time to go inside. "I'm going to go dry off now," she told him, shoving his shoulder playfully as she went by.

"I'll be in soon," he responded as he headed back toward the pile of logs.

While she hung up her coat and shrugged off her boots, the chopping resumed. She was smiling as she entered the kitchen and opened the fridge. Dinner. That had been her intention before she uncharacteristically took a detour.

They were well-stocked again for a while, and she decided on some pork chops and vegetables. She could make rice and maybe turn the vegetables into a stir-fry. How hard could it be?

Half an hour later, Blair glanced up as Dade came through the back door. He was winded, but not too bad considering how hard he'd worked. His face was flushed from the cold.

He startled when he saw her, his eyes going wide before he grinned. "We trading chores?"

She shrugged. "It seemed fair." *It seemed necessary.*

He hooked his coat near the back door and tugged off his boots before wandering in closer. "What are we having for dinner?"

"Probably burnt pork chops and limp vegetables," she joked. "Your wood chopping will make my culinary skills pale in comparison."

He set a hand on her lower back as he leaned over to inhale her stir-fry. "It wasn't a contest."

Her heart rate picked up at the contact and his soft words so close to her ear.

She got so rattled that she accidentally touched the pan with her wrist and then yelped as the pan nearly fell on the floor.

Dade was quick to grab the pan, set it to rights, and turn off the burner while simultaneously tugging her by the forearm over to the sink. He turned on the cold water and held her wrist under the stream.

She didn't think the burn was that bad. Hardly worth the fanfare. Besides, she needed him to step away from her before his proximity made her head spin. Giving a slight jerk, she tried to free herself. "I've got it, Dade."

He didn't release her, though. Instead, he held her steadier, leaning down to see the burn.

"Dade." She pursed her lips, staring at his profile and then his chest and then his grip on her arm. It was too much. She only had so much self-control. It had been teetering for days. Touching her like this was very bad. "Dade," she said louder.

"You need to keep it under the water. Cool it off."

"It's fine." She tugged again.

He ignored her. In fact, he stuck one leg behind her to keep her from backing up, trapping her against the sink.

His biceps brushed against her nipple, making it pebble and sending a shiver down her spine.

She pressed her legs together and bit her lip, willing him to let her go. Arguing was obviously useless. She needed to ride this out until he was appeased.

But he continued to touch her. Too intimately. His fingers rubbed against her arm. Was he even aware?

When he reached with his other hand to uncurl her fist next to the faucet, she reached her breaking point.

With one solid forceful yank of her arm, she jerked out of his grasp. She had too much momentum, however, and windmilled backward, tripping over his foot. She would have fallen on her ass or even hit her head on the table if he hadn't caught her.

He grabbed both her biceps with his hands and steadied her, her back against the edge of the table. "Jesus, Blair. What's up with you? I'm just trying to help."

His face was too close, his body firm and cold from being outside. The length of him pressed against her from thighs to chest.

She lifted her gaze to meet his, so aroused that she wasn't sure she could properly form words. She licked her suddenly dry lips. "Please," she managed.

He cocked his head to one side, confused. "Blair?"

Heart pounding, she couldn't figure out what to say next. Why couldn't he just let her go before she embarrassed herself and put their relationship in jeopardy?

A stare-off ensued. When she couldn't take another second, she made a hard lurch to the right. But Dade was stronger than her. Instead of letting her go, he closed the distance and pressed his lips against hers.

Shocked, at first she didn't return the kiss, but when he tipped his head slightly to one side, making his intentions completely clear, she could no longer stop herself. She'd wanted his lips on hers for so long, she was unable to reason.

He moaned softly into her mouth, his body leaning against hers. She was aware of every inch of him. Cold and warm at the same time. Alert. So aroused. She'd needed this for so many days.

She grabbed his waist, returning the kiss with as much fervor as she felt coming from him. Licking the seam of his lips. Tasting him while he did the same. His grip on her biceps loosened but only because he gradually slid his hands up until one cupped her face and one gripped the back of her neck.

The way he controlled her movements, holding her right where he wanted her, drove her mad. Pent-up desire bubbled from inside as her breasts grew heavy and her sex demanded attention.

Suddenly, he released her. One second he was touching her everywhere, and the next second he was gone.

She blinked her eyes open, swaying to one side, to find his back to her. It wasn't until he turned off the running water that she realized his intention. She took the opportunity to make her escape. But not fast enough.

He returned instantly, shaking his head, hands on her waist, backing her up until she hit the wall. "Nuh-uh. We're not done here." And then he was all over her again. Lips. Hands roaming. One knee nestling between hers. His torso pressing against her breasts. His erection obvious against her belly.

Wetness pooled between her legs as she noted his arousal. He wanted her as badly as she wanted him.

When his hands wormed under her tight-fitting shirt, she sighed into his mouth. The contact of his fingers against her skin sent an urgency through her body. A frantic need to touch his skin, to have him pressed against her. Inside her. Everywhere.

Now.

She fumbled to grab the bottom of his shirt and tug it upward, flattening her palms on his firmness as she smoothed them up to his pecs. Lips still connected, she rose onto her tiptoes to yank his shirt over his head.

His pupils were dilated and intense when he met her gaze as the cotton whipped between their faces. "Blair..." And then he continued devouring her as if they were long-lost lovers reuniting for the first time in years.

She planted her palms on his smooth skin, but was

immediately distracted from her exploration when his hands made their way back under her shirt and over her sports bra.

She was fully aware there was nothing sexy about her undergarments, but based on the way he looked at her every time he saw her working out or walking from or to the equipment room, she doubted he would agree.

He squeezed her breasts, molding his hands to lift and hold them and weigh them, and then he thumbed her nipples. She moaned into his mouth, arching into his touch. He broke the kiss and hastened his efforts to divest her of both her shirt and then her bra, pulling them over her head and dropping them on the floor.

When his gaze landed on her bare chest, she watched his face. His chest rose and fell as time slowed. His hands eased up to cup her breasts again, but this time more reverently. The contact of his thumbs against her nipples was so light she almost didn't notice.

But the tight buds pebbled further.

In the lull, she reached for the button on his jeans, hands shaking with urgency. She fumbled, but he swiped her fingers away and picked her up by the waist. "Legs around me," he demanded. "We're not fucking against this wall."

She complied without a word, loving the feel of his length pushing against her sex. Heady with promise. His words sent flutters to her belly. *Fucking*. It had promise too. Thank God. If he intended to stop this freight train, she might die.

In seconds, she was falling backward until she landed on her bed sideways. He hovered over her, still on his feet, nibbling a path to her ear before pulling back and grabbing the waistband of her leggings. In moments they were gone, leaving her in nothing but a black thong. Not even a sexy lacey one. Just black cotton.

The world stopped spinning again while he scanned her body, worshipping her with his eyes and the tips of his fingers. Learning her. His gaze hesitated on her left arm where her scar was, but only for a second.

Goose bumps rose all over her skin at the intensity of his perusal.

The dancing of his fingertips over her nipples made her fist the comforter at her sides and bite her bottom lip.

A slight furrow in his brow told her he was studying her. It should have unnerved her. Instead, she felt worshipped. He grazed his fingers down her torso next and then hooked them into her thong to draw it off her body. He grabbed her ankles and lifted them, forcing her to bend her knees and causing a moment of self-consciousness as her legs parted to reveal everything.

She held her breath when his hands came to her thighs, holding them wider, thumbs stroking so close to her sex. The cool air in the room made her hyperaware of the gathered wetness.

He inhaled as he lowered his face. "Intoxicating." And then his mouth was on her. Unexpected. Shocking. So good.

She dug her fingers into his shoulders, watching him go down on her, wondering what he thought of the fact that she kept herself groomed bare. Some men liked it. Others didn't. Since it was her body, and she preferred the look and feel, she had shaved everything for most of her adult life.

Dade gave no indication he was disappointed. That was for sure. His lips were on her clit, his tongue flicking over the distended nub so fast her eyes rolled back.

"Dade. Oh, God." She was going to come. Pent-up need rushed to the surface. Too many days of watching him in her space, his presence so all-consuming there was no way to avoid him.

Why had she deprived herself of this man and his talented mouth?

The second he increased the intensity of his sucking and pressed his tongue against her clit, she came. She cried out, something incoherent, while her body rode the waves of pleasure.

It wouldn't stop. Because it wasn't enough. Even after the

orgasm subsided, she was still aroused. Her body begged to be filled. She pressed on his shoulders, hoping to disengage him so that he could take off his jeans.

His gaze was still so intense when he lifted his lips from between her thighs and stared at her.

"Please," she begged, reaching fruitlessly toward his jeans. "Dammit, Dade, I'm going to implode."

He popped the button and lowered the zipper while she watched. The tickets to this show were well worth it as he shimmied out of his jeans and underwear at the same time, leaving himself bare to her gaze.

She should have suspected he would be well-endowed. After all, the rest of him was tall and broad. He was proportionately perfect, which meant his size made her slightly concerned. She'd seen her fair share of erections. Enough to know this one was larger. And she hadn't had sex in a long time.

Suddenly, he froze, his length in his hand. "Shit. I didn't exactly bring condoms. Do you suppose Ryan thought of *everything*?" He glanced at the nightstand.

She shook her head. "I'm clean. It's been a long time. And I'm on the pill."

He smiled, that silly half grin. "I haven't touched a single woman for over a decade."

She rolled her eyes. "Come up here," she demanded as she shoved herself backward to give him space. The bed was enormous. No reason to be dangling off the edge.

He crawled toward her and settled on his side next to her, surprising her with his nonchalance when she was currently feeling an urgency she would expect him to mirror. After all, she'd at least had one orgasm. He had not.

Instead, he propped himself up on his palm, stared down at her, and stroked her neck with his free hand. "I want you to know that I heard what you said earlier." His voice was deep and soft.

She nodded slowly, unsure why he was bringing this up now

or even what he intended to communicate. What she did know was that it seemed important to him, and it endeared him to her. Dammit. Why did he feel the need to add something meaningful to this tryst? Couldn't they just have sex without making a big deal out of it?

As his fingers slid down to toy with her nipple, his gaze followed, but he kept talking. "I'm not intimidated by your strong personality. In fact, it's attractive. I don't know why anyone who spent even five minutes with you wouldn't want to get to know you better."

"Well, I have my own reasons for not wanting to encourage anyone to get close to me." She pursed her lips after those words slipped out, hoping he wouldn't press her for more information. The last thing she wanted to do at the moment was be psychoanalyzed.

He lifted his gaze back to hers but said nothing for several seconds. His next words headed in a different direction. "I'm pretty sure I swallowed my tongue the first time you spoke. Do you remember what you said to me?"

She nodded, seriously concerned about the depth of this little chat. She had been physically attracted to him since the day they met, but she didn't want to get so deeply emotionally involved that he had the ability to break her heart.

Forget the possibility that he might die. She could handle death. What she worried about was the probability that he might walk away from her any day if his damn ego got in the way and he decided it would be best for her. Especially now. Especially since he'd seen her naked. Especially after he finally slid inside her.

She realized he was watching her, waiting for words to go with her nod. "I said, 'It's not a bad idea, you know.'" She would never forget that moment.

He smiled. "It was corny, but you got my attention." He inhaled deeply. "What I'm trying to say is, any man who could walk away from you would have to be extremely insecure with himself.

Strong women should not repel a man." He leaned his face closer and nibbled a path to her ear.

She shivered.

"I don't care if you're bossy in the bedroom or not. Feel free to do so any time you want. But I'm also going to enjoy making you scream. Can you handle that?" His top leg slid between hers, nudging her knees apart, his thigh pressing against her heat.

She didn't answer him. She couldn't.

Instead, she reached for him with her unpinned hand, threading her fingers with his over her breast.

When he pinched her nipple exquisitely, she arched into him and moaned. *Please. Oh, God, please...*

CHAPTER 12

Dade was mesmerized. Blair hadn't said much while he rambled on probably incoherently, trying to tell her that he didn't care if she was dominant or submissive in the bedroom. It wasn't a deal breaker for him either way. And in his opinion, it shouldn't have been for any other man either.

He had no idea if she had a dominant side in bed, but he suspected from her words earlier and her actions now, that she at least got off on him leading.

With her fingers tucked around his, he slid his hand down her belly and reached between her legs. She started to pull her hand away when he stroked his middle finger over her clit, but he stopped her. "Leave it. Shadow me while I touch you."

She sucked in a sharp breath but didn't attempt to draw away again.

He was so hard it was growing difficult to concentrate, but he wanted to bring her back to the edge before he entered her.

She had no idea how sexy she was every minute of every day, but right now she was so much more. He kept glancing at her face, memorizing the way her emotions were written all over. Her cheeks were flushed. Her blue eyes darker than usual. Her pupils wide.

She had a look of desperation, and yet she didn't ask him to take her, nor did she give any indication she might flip roles on him and take for herself.

When he pressed one finger up inside her, taking her own finger with him, she gasped, her mouth falling open and her eyes rolling back. He dragged his finger over her G-spot, and when he noticed how her belly dipped as he did so, he did it again.

She was so responsive to everything he did. It made him harder by the second to know he did this to her. He drove her to this edge. This place that put that look of sheer bliss on her face.

"Blair, look at me."

She blinked, trying to focus on him.

He smiled. "God, you're gorgeous when you're aroused. You sure you want this?" He wasn't playing fair asking her that while he flicked the tip of his finger over her G-spot, the palm of his hand pressing against her clit. "Tell me to stop and I will." He was harder than hell. Stopping would kill him if anemia didn't. But he had always been extremely careful to make sure what headspace every one of his lovers was in the first time he had sex with them.

She frowned, confused. "Are you asking me if I want you to make love to me? Is it not obvious? Do I seem reluctant or uninterested?"

He slowly smiled. Maybe she had more of her wits than he thought. She was quite coherent. "Is that a yes?" he teased, to see what she would do next.

She dropped her head back and groaned. "Dade Menke, I'm still stronger than you. Don't make me hurt you."

He knew she meant those words to infer what she might do to him later. Right now, she made no aggressive moves. She wanted him to take her. And he had never been so pleased.

After pulling both of their fingers out of her, he drew them to his mouth to suck her sweetness from their combined hands.

Releasing her, he climbed between her legs as he propped his elbows near her shoulders. His erection lined up with her entrance as if there were a magnetic pull between them.

He lowered his lips to hers and claimed her mouth in a slow kiss, his chest brushing against her amazing breasts as he eased himself into her.

Damn, she was tight. Apparently it had been a long time for both of them. He had to release her lips to concentrate, or he would come too soon.

It was hard to hold her gaze, but the emotion he saw in her eyes was mesmerizing. Her lips parted as he inched deeper, and she gasped when he finally thrust the rest of the way into her tight channel.

He held still, fighting against the need to come. *Shit. Oh, God.* He was losing the battle. Even without moving, he struggled to stop the rush of blood to his erection.

"Dade, please..." Her sweet voice urged him to move. Releasing his breath, he pulled almost fully out and thrust back in. Every slide of his length against her stretched channel was a victory. He squeezed his eyes closed, concentrating on the feel of her, the way her breath hit his lips, the way the tight pebbles of her nipples grazed his chest, the way her thighs hugged his...

Bliss.

He picked up the speed as the pressure and need intensified. She would understand his lack of stamina. He would make it up to her later.

When he couldn't stop it another second, he thrust deep one last time and released a groan as the pulses of his orgasm took him to heaven.

Spent, he lowered his forehead to the mattress next to her temple, holding her tight. He was aware she hadn't come a second time, and he fully intended to rectify that as soon as he could move.

She squirmed beneath the pressure of his body, undoubtedly needing to come.

"Hold still, baby," he encouraged next to her ear. "Give me one second. I'll get you there."

She moaned. Her hands were on his waist, and they smoothed around to cup his ass and squeeze. "It's okay," she whispered. "I'm fine."

She was not fine by a longshot. He could tell by her breathing, the disconnect in her words, and the way her body wouldn't still.

The second he could move, he lifted one leg to straddle her thigh, let his length slide out of her, and landed on his side next to her. When he pressed his thigh against her sex, she gasped. He smiled against the side of her face, knowing she couldn't see him. There was nothing sexier than a woman on the verge of an orgasm.

His fingers were shaking, but he smoothed his hand down her belly and wiggled it between his thigh and her warmth.

Her breath hitched beautifully when he touched her sensitive clit. As he circled the swollen nub, he propped his head up to watch her face. She grabbed his forearm, though he doubted she had any idea if she was pulling or pushing him away. It didn't matter. He was strong enough to hold his ground.

Circling her clit made her hold her breath. Tapping it made her wiggle her butt. Flicking it made her moan. So, he did all three, watching her as she grew closer to the edge. He knew she was there when her heels dug into the bed and she attempted to lift her torso off the mattress.

And then she came.

He flattened his fingers against her clit so he could feel the pulses of her orgasm, mesmerized by the experience as if he too were feeling the waves of pleasure. In a way, he was. By extension.

Her body collapsed like Jell-O against the bed when the orgasm passed.

He hated for the moment to end. He wanted to continue

watching her as she came down from the high, but his body was too heavy and sated to comply, so he dropped his cheek next to hers and tucked her against his side.

As his heart rate returned to normal, he realized he was in deep dog doo-doo. Blair Rollans was not just some woman he had sex with. This had been special. Amazing. Life-altering.

Fuck.

They lay there for a long time, both breathing heavily. He could feel her heartbeat against his palm between her breasts. When she lifted her hand and set it on top of his, a sense of peace and contentment spread throughout his body.

"Dinner was probably burnt before you turned off the stove. I can't imagine what it must look like now." She giggled, the sound musical.

He kissed her shoulder. That was as far as he could move at the moment. "It'll be fine. If not, we'll toss it."

"Give me a minute to recover, and I'll go check. As soon as my legs start receiving messages from my brain."

He stroked the space between her breasts with his fingers. "No rush. Relax. Don't move yet. I like you right here. Besides, your mattress is amazing. I might fall asleep and never miss dinner."

She twisted her face to see him. "You said the one in the other room was fine."

"I lied." He grinned.

Her eyes widened. "Why would you do that?"

"Because I didn't want you to give up your room or order a mattress or something crazy and unnecessary."

She sighed. "Martyr."

He chuckled. "Maybe."

She smoothed her hand over his, stroking the back of his. "We just had sex."

"We did. You okay?"

"I'm more worried about you."

"Me?" He lifted his head a few inches to see her expression

more fully. "You've been dating some strange guys if they've had regrets after sex," he joked. When did this get so serious? *The moment you slid into her.*

She rolled her eyes. "First of all, I haven't dated many guys at all, so it would be difficult to use the short list as a test group. But I can tell you that none of the men I've been with currently believed they were dying, nor did any of them need protection against an unknown enemy who might want them dead. So, yes. I'm more worried about you."

He groaned. "Look at this from my point of view instead. I've never had sex with a woman knowing full well I was going to die on her and that I was putting her life in danger just by spending time with her."

"See? We have a difference of opinion. I'm a trained professional bodyguard, so not a chance someone is going to off me. And you're not dying."

"You find a cure for AA2 while I was out chopping wood?"

"Yes. Optimism."

He rolled onto his back, wishing like hell they hadn't spoken at all. He'd been so relaxed beside her and even inside her. Why did they have to go back to this place where she insisted on keeping an unreasonably optimistic view while he scrambled to find a way to live? "You do realize good vibes, incense, and prayer are not going to fix my malfunctioning bone marrow, right?"

She rolled to her side, propped her head on her hand, and looked down at him. "Of course, but an improved drug, a bone marrow transplant, or the stem cell thing might work. I prefer to have hope."

He turned his head away from her and closed his eyes. He never should have slept with her. What was he thinking? Now she was going to be even worse than before with her optimism.

"Now what?" she asked, exasperated.

He shifted his gaze to face her again. "I prefer to live in the real world. I'm not the kind of person who's going to paste on a smile and pretend life is great when the truth is, I'm probably going to die in a few months. If you spend all that time pretending that isn't my reality, it will annoy me."

Maybe he shouldn't have been so blunt. The words tumbled out of his mouth without him thinking them through first. He might have sounded a little harsh.

"Fine." She rolled away from him and climbed off the opposite side of the bed. After snatching her clothes off the floor, she stomped to the bathroom and shut the door.

"Dammit," he muttered. Nothing like a pissing off a woman right after having sex. *Good job, Dade.*

He pushed off the bed and grabbed his jeans from the floor. He was just zipping them up when she came back out of the bathroom wearing those damn leggings and a new T-shirt.

As she walked by him, she mumbled something about checking the food.

He followed her to the kitchen, barefoot, jeans, no shirt. "Blair..."

She shook her head to deny him. "Don't. Let it go. Let's eat." After peering into the pans, she grabbed plates. She must have determined her cooking looked edible because she filled a plate and then stepped around him without touching him to go sit in her favorite chair in the living room.

Dade took a deep breath and filled another plate. It smelled good. It was cold, but he didn't think it was ruined from either her cooking or from the passage of time. He followed her to the living room and plopped down on the couch, but he couldn't imagine swallowing. His chest was tight from arguing with her.

He couldn't stand the idea of making her angry with him, but he also couldn't picture weeks on end of her pretending he wasn't sick. He wasn't convinced any of the options to save his life would work.

Ten years ago, he'd devoted every waking moment to finding a cure for AP12, racing against the clock to save his own life. Fate was a cruel bitch to have him wake up a decade later only to repeat the same frantic search for AA2. What did he do in a past life to deserve this?

One thing he knew for sure was that he indeed needed to regroup and get his head in the game. He didn't have time to play around. It wouldn't do any good to develop a relationship with Blair if in the end he died because he was busy having sex instead of researching anemia.

He needed to find more studies. He needed to get back to work.

He needed more time.

Blair was going to be a distraction. More now than ever, especially if she got the idea that just because they'd had sex, he was going to move into her bed and spend long leisurely hours fucking. He couldn't afford to do that.

He needed to be alone somewhere where he could work undistracted until he either figured out a solution or died trying. Resolved, he glanced at her to find her eyeing him suspiciously. She probably knew he was about to speak. "I think it would be better if I wasn't here."

CHAPTER 13

For a moment, the air in the room stood still. And then Blair's plate slid to the floor and she jumped to her feet. "You selfish asshole," she shouted.

His eyes went wide as he set his plate on the coffee table and then leaned back with his hands on his thighs. "What?" He knew she was pissed off, but he didn't understand this reaction at all.

She stomped toward him, anger turning her cheeks red. "You don't fucking get to decide that."

He flinched as she got closer. "Decide what?"

"Don't look at me like it's no big deal. Don't even joke about something like that. It infuriates me when people make such flippant comments." She leaned over him, shaking a finger in his face, furious. "It's never too late. I don't care if you're sorry we had sex. Fine. If you want to go back to the way things were before, fine. If you're scared, fine. If you want to work night and day looking for a cure, fine. I'll help or stay out of your way or hand you food or whatever you need. But don't ever, ever fucking say something like that again."

He opened his mouth to speak, but he didn't know what to say. Her rambling stream of words made no sense to him.

She kept talking. "You're not even sick. You're perfectly healthy right now. I just experienced firsthand how healthy you are." She flung a finger toward the bedroom as if he needed the reminder of what had happened in there so very recently.

"Blair—"

She shook her head rapidly and cut him off. "No. You listen to me. I realize I'm acting like a lunatic, and I have my reasons. I'm extremely sensitive about this subject. Irrational or not. Don't. Ever. Fucking. Mention. Suicide. Again. Got it?"

He startled in his seat. "Suicide? Who said anything about suicide?" Was that what this was all about?

She stopped bending so close to him and righted herself. "You did."

He shook his head. "No. I didn't. I think I suggested that I leave. I meant the cabin. Not the earth."

Her face turned a deep red so fast, and she stumbled backward. He thought she might fall, but when he stood to grab her flailing arms, she jumped back, turned around, and left the room again.

He watched her, more confused than ever.

She didn't shut the door to her room, which he considered significant.

For several moments he stood right where he was, trying to make sense of her rant and what he should do next. Obviously, she had misunderstood his words. And also obviously, the subject of suicide made her lose her shit. This wasn't the first time she'd misunderstood him and reacted violently to thinking he might take his own life. There was a story behind that.

Finally, he followed her, leaving their still uneaten food in the living room—hers all over the floor, his on the coffee table. He found her curled on her side on the far end of the rumpled bed. He ignored the messy comforter that represented to him an amazing hour of his life.

He wasn't exactly the king of soothing a woman's feelings. In fact, he couldn't remember a single time in his life when he'd had to confront someone like this, but he damn well had to now. He had inadvertently contributed to the misunderstanding by constantly bitching about his situation and expressing a complete lack of hope.

He sat on the edge of the bed next to her but didn't touch her. "Blair, I'm sorry."

"Not your fault," she whispered. "I'm sorry too."

"Talk to me." He hoped she understood that he wanted her to open up and throw him a bone here.

Her eyes were closed, and she looked the most vulnerable he'd ever seen her, curled onto her side, her face smashed into the pillow, her hands fisted in front of her chest. This was not his Blair.

"My sister committed suicide." Her words were barely audible.

He stopped breathing.

"She was fourteen. I found her myself in the tub. She slit her wrists."

"Oh, God. Blair..." There were no words. He lifted a hand and set it gently on her thigh, hoping she wouldn't brush him away. Thankfully, she did not. Tears fell down her face now.

"So selfish. She knew I would find her. It was our shared bathroom. For years I was angry with her. It took a lot of therapy for me to see things through her eyes. It still pisses me off. I took it out on you. I'm sorry."

"Baby, it's understandable. If I had known, I would have chosen my words more carefully." He leaned toward her nightstand and grabbed a tissue, handing it to her.

She took it and wiped her eyes. "I haven't told anyone about Jen in years."

Damn. That was huge. He felt privileged, but also a little nervous. "I'm honored, and I swear I would never do something like that. I will fight to the end. I promise."

She reached out with one hand and grabbed his where it sat in front of her. Her grip was strong. He squeezed her fingers in return, running his other hand up and down her thigh. "I loved her so much. She was the most important person in my life. She understood me better than anyone, and then she left me."

My God. He realized how much baggage she had been carrying around for much of her life. It even occurred to him that she probably kept people at arm's length because she didn't want to get too close to them. It would hurt too badly if anything happened to someone else she loved. She knew it firsthand. And Dade was going to leave her too. Just like her sister had.

Shit.

He held his breath as those thoughts hit him hard. He could do nothing to keep from hurting her, just as he'd suspected all along. And now he'd slept with her to make things worse.

Would he take it back if he could? He didn't think so. And he doubted she would either. The pain was real and in their faces, but they also had feelings for each other. A mutual attraction they had denied for too long.

Taking a risk, he slid his hand up her back while he climbed over her and spooned her body from behind. He wrapped his arm around her torso tight and held her close. There wasn't anything else to say.

Yeah, this woman had wormed her way into his heart, intentionally or otherwise. Now what was he going to do to protect her from more of the hurt she was already experiencing? If she felt this badly almost twenty years after her sister died, how would she feel after he passed if they got too close?

He didn't have answers, but he also couldn't walk away from her, so he closed his eyes and tried to relax, holding this precious woman in his arms.

Dade startled awake at the sound of a crash.

He bolted upright, trying to get his bearings as fast as possible. Glancing around, he realized he was in Blair's room on her bed, and she was no longer next to him.

She appeared in the doorway moments later. "Shit. I'm so sorry. I dropped a pan. Did I scare you?"

He ran a hand through his hair as he swung his legs off the side of the bed and went toward her. "Not going to lie. Yes." He followed her into the kitchen as she retreated.

"I have no idea how bad that meal was the first time we were supposed to eat it, and it was probably far worse the second time we didn't eat it. So, I cleaned it up and threw it all away. How about grilled cheese?" She forced a smile as she faced him.

She was so flustered, it was kinda sweet.

He approached, noticing the kitchen was totally clean. She had been in the process of starting over. It was late, but his stomach was rumbling now that he was up. Grilled cheese would be perfect. He crowded her, hating that she kept avoiding him.

When he had her backed into the corner of the kitchen between the sink and the stove, he set one hand on either side of her body on the counter. "Look at me."

She fidgeted but finally met his gaze, her smile fake.

"We had sex."

She nodded.

"It was fantastic."

She nodded again.

"We don't have to do it again if it makes you uncomfortable."

She bit her lip.

He was making this up on the fly here. Honestly, this was not the speech he had planned before he fell asleep. He should be either avoiding the fact that they slept together and pretending it didn't happen or telling her they couldn't do it again. Instead, he was giving her options. What the hell?

But she was vulnerable. And cute as fuck. Flustered. Nervous.

She didn't do things like this. She didn't sleep with men casually like it was no big deal. He was certain of it.

"I don't know what to say," she whispered.

"You don't have to say anything, but I don't want us to tiptoe around for days on end pretending it didn't happen or feel too uncomfortable to discuss it." He couldn't do that to her. Maybe in his past life he could have blown off a woman without thinking twice, but not in this life. Not with this woman. He would be an ass to do so.

"'Kay."

He needed to touch her, so he stepped closer, closing the gap between them, and wrapped his arms around her to pull her into his embrace. With his face buried in her hair, he spoke near her ear. "I'm so sorry about your sister. That has to hurt. You can trust me. I won't do that to you."

She nodded, tipping her forehead into his chest.

He kissed the top of her head. "Now, grilled cheese sounds amazing, but in the interest of saving bread and not wasting cheese, why don't you let me make it? After all, we don't know how long it will be until someone brings us more supplies."

She leaned back, punched his chest playfully, and met his gaze with a smile. "That's not funny."

He smirked. "It kinda is."

She giggled. "Okay, yeah. It is. You're right. You make the grilled cheese. I'll just go sit at the table and look pretty." She ducked under his arm and fled.

He turned around as she hoisted onto a stool. "That won't be hard."

"Be serious."

He frowned. "I am."

"Whatever."

He strolled closer, intent on setting her straight on this topic also. "I know you have a tough act you present to the world, and I know you think it repels people, but let me tell you a few things." He crowded her again, setting his hands on her shoulders.

Her face was closer to his with her sitting up on the stool. She looked uncomfortable, glancing away from him.

"First of all, Tough Blair is sexy as hell. Only an asshole would find it intimidating or repelling, so you can kick that misconception out the door now. Second of all, I'm going to bet that few people have ever seen the totally feminine sexy woman who lives under that tough exterior. But I have. And I'm humbled to count myself among those few."

She blushed.

He slid a hand up to cup her face and tip her head back. "So, yeah, you can sit over here and look pretty because you can't help it. You have no other choice. Even Tough Blair in a uniform with a bun and no makeup and an axe is hot as hell. The woman who thinks she looks no different in tight leggings and sports bras is sadly mistaken." He leaned closer, kissed her nose, and then held her gaze at a few inches. "That woman is on fire."

She wasn't breathing.

He felt victorious. So, he kissed her forehead next and then released her to head for the fridge.

"What would you do if I came out of my room in a silk nightie or wore a black lacey bra and panty set under a skintight dress?"

He released the refrigerator door before grabbing anything and spun around. "So, you have those things?" he asked before he could stop himself. His mouth was literally watering.

She shrugged, sending him a coy look. "Maybe. Maybe not."

He swallowed. "Woman." His jeans got too tight. "You're killing me," he murmured as he returned to the fridge. Without looking at her, he pulled out everything he would need and turned toward the stove. He made himself concentrate on the sandwiches and ignore his arousal and the fact that he knew she was staring at him.

When he thought he finally had himself composed and the

sandwiches were browning in the pan, he finally turned around. Indeed, she was watching him.

"If you want to get anything done around here, I suggest you not run around the cabin with no shirt on. It's distracting."

He smirked again. "We're back to that again?"

She nodded. "How does a man who's been in a cryostat for ten years come out with pecs like that?"

He glanced down as if he were unfamiliar with his own chest. "These?" He pointed at them. "I've never seen them before. They were just there when I woke up from my coma."

"Ha-ha. Good one."

He turned back around to flip the sandwiches. Moments later, he had them on the plates and carried them to the table. As he set them down, he slid a hand up her arm and glanced at her chest. "How does a woman who's been hiding from men for far more than ten years not realize her body is perfection?"

She licked her lips and then shocked him with her response. "Thank you." No eye roll. No groan. No denial. Just *thank you*.

"You're welcome." He slid into the chair next to her.

"Do you think that's what I've been doing? Hiding?"

He lifted half a grilled cheese and glanced sideways at her. "Haven't you?"

She faced her plate and toyed with the crust. "Maybe. I've been told that before. But I don't do it consciously."

He took a bite, a string of cheese running from the sandwich to his mouth. He had to break it with his fingers. After swallowing, he faced her again. "Maybe you're afraid to let people get close? I'm no psychiatrist, mind you, but if you've been hurting that badly since your sister died, maybe you're leery about loving people for fear they will leave you."

When she blinked, he knew he'd struck a nerve. She was more than aware she pushed people away for that very reason. "You sure you're not a psychiatrist? I've heard that a few times from several of them."

He smiled. "Just observing."

She sighed. "The truth is, it's probably deeper than that. It goes back a little further. My mom wasn't very present in our lives. She was distant. I'd say she was a high-functioning alcoholic. She wasn't touchy-feely. She rarely hugged us. She didn't play with us.

"When my sister died, she got even worse. More distant. My dad always carried most of the weight, before and after. It took him a long time to reconnect with the world after Jen died. I talk to him every few weeks nowadays. I haven't spoken to my mom in months."

"Damn. That must be hard."

She nodded, eating some more of her sandwich. "This is really good," she pointed out as she swallowed and took a drink of water.

He nudged her with his shoulder. "It's not burnt."

She shoved him back with a hand. "If you keep it up, I'll never enter the kitchen again. It's all yours."

"At least that way we won't starve," he joked.

She looked back at her plate. Several seconds went by. He was worried he'd gone too far. But when she spoke again, she was back on the subject of her mom. "I think I didn't learn how to love properly. I mean, I loved my sister, but it wasn't enough, so it affected me."

"That makes sense." He hurt inside for the sixteen-year-old girl who found her dead sister in the bathtub. No one should have to endure that.

"I was so angry. Violently so. With Jen. With my mom... I barely held it together until I graduated. That's when I decided to join the army. It was the perfect thing for me to do. Enlist. The hard work and discipline helped heal me in a way. Or at least it kept my mind off my problems by filling my time with the grueling tasks of an enlisted woman."

He shoved his plate back and swiveled his stool to face her, his legs spread so that she was between them. He grabbed the back of her chair. "You're an amazing woman. Stronger than anyone I know. And I don't mean physically. Emotionally too."

She played with the last piece of bread on her plate.

"It all makes more sense to me now. Thank you for sharing."

"I'll clean up," she whispered.

"How about you go to bed. You're exhausted. I'll do it."

She lifted her gaze to him and hesitated. "How about you come with me. I plopped down on your mattress earlier and nearly fell through to China. Stop sleeping in that bed. Mine is a king. It's big enough for three of us."

He lifted a brow. "You planning on inviting a third?" he teased.

"Never. I can barely handle one man. No way would I want two."

"Who said the third had to be a man?" he joked.

"Touché." She laughed as she walked away from him.

Dade tossed the few dishes they'd used in the dishwasher and turned out the lights. He headed for his bedroom first to change into flannel sleep pants, and then he used his bathroom.

When he stepped back into the hallway, she was leaning at the entrance to her room. She had on loose cotton shorts and a tank top that should have been illegal. "I meant what I said about sleeping in my bed. I'm not trying to pressure you. Don't think of it like I asked you to move in with me after one date or anything. It just makes good sense. You'll sleep better on a better mattress. I'll sleep better knowing you're safe next to me."

"Safe?" he asked as he approached, fighting the urge to stare at her chest. How were her boobs that fucking perfect and high without a bra? "From myself or bad guys?"

"Both?"

He lifted a hand and stroked her cheek. "I made you a promise. I won't renege." He knew how badly it would destroy her if someone else she was close to committed suicide. He couldn't do that to her even if it had ever crossed his mind.

"Okay, then do it because it will be more comfortable."

"How about I do it because the woman in the bed with me makes my blood pump?"

"Or for that reason. Whatever works."

He chuckled, took her hand, and led her toward the bed. "You going to stay on your side?"

"If you want me to."

He was feeling her out. She was giving him almost no indication where she stood on the issue of their relationship. He pulled her toward one side, sat on the edge of the mattress, and positioned her between his legs. "We're both exhausted, and I know you're uncertain, so let's get some sleep, okay? Things don't have to be weird between us."

She nodded, lifting both hands to cup his face. "They're not weird, just awkward. You can't possibly tell me you aren't uncertain too."

"You're right. But I think we have different motives holding us back. No matter what, sleeping in the same bed won't change anything. I'll sleep better if I can reach out and touch you. You'll sleep better if you can hear me breathing next to you."

"Yes."

He slid his hands up her back and pulled her the last few inches so he could gently kiss her lips.

The fact that she didn't flinch or turn away spoke volumes.

Easing her a few steps back, he pulled the comforter down, slid into the bed, and scooted back several feet so she could join him. He lifted a hand in invitation.

She flipped off the light on the nightstand and climbed into his embrace.

His body relaxed as he pulled her back against his chest. He didn't say anything, but his mind was racing. It felt so good holding her. The ten days he'd spent with her nearly nonstop seemed like months or years. He knew she was awake, but he couldn't think of anything to say that wouldn't sound sappy, so he stroked her forearm between her breasts instead.

She snuggled closer in response.

Could they somehow make this weird thing between them okay? He couldn't decide if sleeping with her had been the best idea of his life or the worst mistake. Time would tell. He certainly couldn't take it back. What he should do was back up a few steps and give her space.

It would be weird to presume that just because they had sex once, they were automatically in a relationship that dictated they should spend their days lying around naked and feeding each other grapes. That wasn't his style anyway, but he also had a disease to cure.

Tomorrow, he intended to get up and attempt a new normal. He wouldn't push their encounter under the rug and ignore it, but he would step back and let her make the next move. After all, she was the one who stood to lose in this game. A lot. The least he could do would be to give her the time she needed to consider what getting romantically involved with him would mean for the long run.

When her breathing evened out, he finally relaxed enough to clear his mind and fall into a deep sleep.

CHAPTER 14

Blair awoke to the smell of bacon. She smiled as she rolled onto her back and stared at the ceiling. How long had he been up? She must have been incredibly tired to have slept through their disentanglement and him leaving the room.

After a quick trip to the bathroom, she padded toward the kitchen.

Dade had not only been up a while, but he'd already worked out. She could tell by the line of sweat running down the back of his T-shirt. Sexy as hell.

He turned around, a smile crossing his face when he spotted her. She leaned one hip against the cabinets next to the fridge. "You sleep well?" he asked.

"For the first time in a long time, yes. You?"

"Like a baby."

"I hear babies don't really sleep that well."

He chuckled. "I've never actually been around one."

"Me neither. Except my sister, but I was two." How did they get on this subject? Jeez. She'd never thought much about having kids. She'd spent most of her adult life avoiding men. That wasn't conducive to having a baby. It hadn't been a phase of life she'd thought about often. She'd simply assumed she would never get married and left it at that.

As she watched Dade turn back to face the stove, she pondered a different world in which she spent her life with someone like him and they had kids together.

Maybe it wouldn't be that bad. Maybe if Dade was hers, she could take that kind of step. He was the sort of man who would share the burden. That was for sure.

Even after spending less than two weeks with him, she knew he would always share any burden with her or take on more for himself. Chopping wood. Cooking. Even research. He didn't make a big deal out of anything. He simply divided the workload in a way that suited them and made it happen. He was nothing like any man she'd ever dated.

"You okay?" he asked, startling her.

"Yes. Sure. Sorry. My mind wandered."

"Did it go someplace interesting?" he asked, as he filled plates and set them on the table.

"What? No. Just random thoughts." No way would she tell him she was visualizing the two of them leaning over an imaginary crib. He would freak out worse than he already had.

When he shot her a curious glance, she changed the subject. "So, what's on the research schedule for today?" she asked, as she slid onto a stool.

"I made you a list." He pointed at the other side of the table toward a piece of paper next to the second computer Ryan had brought them yesterday.

"Damn, you have been up a while."

"Like I said, I slept hard. For the first time since we got here. It's a wonder my back survived that other mattress."

"Like I said, martyr. What kind of fool suffers night after night on a shitty mattress for no good reason?"

"The kind of fool who knew there was no way he could avoid

stealing the virtue of the woman in the other bed if he climbed in next to her."

She laughed. "Virtue? What year is it? It's true that I haven't had many boyfriends, but I wasn't a virgin."

"Figure of speech. It sounded better than if I had said I would have fucked you sooner."

"True."

"I've been thinking. We need to find a way to get my grandfather's money."

She nodded and then picked up her fork. "I agree. You never know how much it might be. You could take a vacation or something." She sounded silly.

He frowned. "Do I seem like the kind of guy who plans to take a vacation right now?"

"No," she conceded. "But maybe after you get the treatment. You can't do anything while you're contagious."

"So, between the treatment and my imminent death."

"Dade..."

"Sorry. I'll try not to be snarky about it, but it's hard. I think I toss it around like that partly because I'm being realistic and partly because I'm scared out of my mind."

She stopped eating to look at him.

He didn't meet her gaze, however. Instead, he pushed food around his plate.

She slid out of her seat and came around to his side of the table. When she reached him, she spun him to the side. Seconds later her arms were around him, and he was hugging her back fiercely.

"It's okay to be scared. I am too."

He nodded against her. "Give me some time to adjust. It was hard to face before we slept together. Now I'm experiencing another level of stress entirely."

"I'm sorry. I didn't mean to contribute to your stress." It made her chest squeeze to think of her part in his burden.

He eased her back and met her gaze. "You didn't. Don't ever think that. I need you to understand that my anxiety has little to do with a fear of dying. I'm not really worried about that. I'm scared to death thinking about how badly it's going to hurt you. I never wanted this to happen. I tried to keep us at arm's length. I thought if we didn't get close, it would help you move on easier."

She gave him a shake. "I'm sick and tired of hearing that. It wouldn't have mattered if you'd ignored me for the past week or if you'd *married* me a week ago. I still wouldn't want anything to happen to you. I may be tough on the outside, but I'm not unfeeling on the inside.

"I care about you. If anything ever happened to you for any reason, it would hurt. You can't stop it by trying to spare me grief. In fact, if you think it would help to backpedal now, you're wrong." She didn't want to pressure him in any way. He needed to be the one to decide how involved he was willing to go with her. Especially because he was the one whose life was at stake.

His brow furrowed. "I'm trying to see things your way. I really am. Give me time. I'm not convinced I'm not hurting you more by the minute."

She needed to say one more thing, even though it was only going to make his stress increase. She stepped closer, kissed him briefly but boldly on the lips, and then she cleared her throat. "You will be hurting me if you turn your back on me. I'll step back and give you all the space you need. And I understand you have to spend the majority of every day with your head so deep inside that computer that you don't even know I'm in the room. That's understandable. But if you get cold on me and pull away at other times of the day and night, that will hurt. I want this. I want to be with you."

"Noted."

"Good. Now, eat your breakfast so you'll have the energy to cure a disease." She started to pull away, but he hauled her back.

For several seconds, he just stared at her, his eyes thoughtful, and then he slowly drew her in closer and kissed her more completely. When he pulled back, he glanced down. "I'll do my best to find a cure for AA2, but I'm gonna need you to put on more clothes."

She rolled her eyes. "You're so fixated on what I wear. I'm covered. Shirt. Shorts." She nodded toward her chest, noticing how tight her tank top was and that her nipples were pebbled. Maybe he had a point this time.

He lifted a brow. "I'm usually a serious man fully capable of concentrating on my work without distraction, but you try me. Every day."

"Every day?" Why did that make her giddy?

"Every day." He slid his hands down her back and gave her butt a squeeze. "I'll make you a deal. You go work out after breakfast while I get started on research. If you come back fully covered, I promise to divest you of every stitch later tonight like a gift wrapped up for me."

She chuckled. "You're such a man."

He swatted her butt as she stepped away. "You're just now noticing?"

It was afternoon when Blair's phone rang, and she snatched it up quickly to keep from disturbing Dade. She even eased out of the kitchen quietly as she connected.

The caller was Tushar, and she had barely said hello before he asked to speak to Dade.

"Sure. Hang on." She turned back around and came to Dade's side, setting a hand on his shoulder as she often did to get his attention slowly without startling him.

He glanced up.

She held out the phone. "Tushar."

He took it from her and leaned back in the chair as she headed for the fridge to grab a bottle of water. When she turned around, he was nodding, but his face was pale. He also wasn't looking at her. He was staring out the window. "Uh-huh... Okay... No, I get it... All right... We'll talk again then... Sure... Bye." He set the phone on the table slowly, took a long deep breath, and then lowered his head back to the laptop without acknowledging her.

She didn't want to be nosey, but what the hell? His reaction had been strange. She also knew Ryan had taken a blood sample yesterday, so she wasn't crazy to worry about what the results might show. Did they already have results?

Whatever Tushar had said to Dade, he obviously didn't want to talk about it, so she decided to leave him alone for now. Let him process. He was already typing rapidly again.

He didn't speak for the rest of the afternoon, but that wasn't unusual. They did this every day. Now that they had two computers, they didn't even need to switch places and discuss whose turn it was to use the iPad.

At six thirty, she headed for the kitchen, wondering if she should attempt to cook something or remind him that it was late.

He must have sensed her because the laptop closed and he stood. "Shit. I didn't realize how late it was. We need to eat."

"Yep." She was staring into the fridge, hoping he would take over this task.

He grabbed the door and eased it open farther, not touching her or looking at her. "I've got it."

"You sure? I could help. Give me a task." She stepped out of the way so he could pull out everything he needed for whatever he had in mind.

When it seemed he'd rather work alone, she leaned against the counter to watch him work. Sometimes he was as zoned while cooking as he could get while researching. Today was worse.

Radio silence.

It was still fascinating to watch him work. He had so many things happening at once but so perfectly timed that everything was finished at the same moment. She loved watching him, both working and cooking. And chopping wood. And resting. And lifting weights.

She loved watching him.

Was he sick?

She feared the answer, but the elephant in the room was crowding the space.

She waited until they were done eating and had the kitchen cleaned. She waited some more because he left the room without a word after hardly saying a thing at dinner. She waited some more while he took a shower in his bathroom and she got ready for bed.

There wasn't much else to do at night in the dark in this cabin. She usually liked to curl up with a book. Tonight, she wouldn't be able to read if she wanted to, but she held it in front of her anyway, pretending while she listened closely for Dade to turn off the shower, brush his teeth, and finally join her.

He sighed as he headed to the other side of the bed. "Why am I so tired? It's only eight thirty." His back was to her.

A knot formed in her throat as he slid under the covers, several feet…and two thousand miles from her.

He stared at the ceiling.

She set her book aside, turned off the light, and crawled across the bed to reach him. No way in hell was she going to let this go. Luckily, when she eased against his side, he wrapped his arm around her and kissed the top of her head.

"Talk to me," she whispered.

"Not much to say."

"Say it anyway."

"It started."

"Okay." She figured that. "So we deal with it. What are the first symptoms?"

"Fatigue. Dizziness. Pallor. Headaches. Numbness."

Her chest tightened. She tried not to react outwardly. "I assume it will be gradual?"

"Yes, but we have no way of knowing how slow or fast." He smashed his face against her hair, breathing deeply.

She had to fight the tears that wanted to escape. Dealing with her sadness wouldn't be fair to him. She needed to be strong. "So what do we do?"

"Nothing yet. Someone will come out and take another blood sample in a week and see what changes have occurred. There are medicines that will buy me time."

Buy him time... God, she hated this. She had hoped to have months before this day came. It hadn't even been two weeks. She sucked back her own concerns. "I'm here."

He held her tighter. "I know." Gradually his grip loosened as he started to relax.

"Are you considering the stem cell transplant?"

"It's a possibility. We'll watch the changes closely for a few weeks to see how quickly the symptoms progress."

She nodded and lay awake with her head in the crook of his arm for hours, breathing in his scent, enjoying the feeling of being held, worrying that what they'd had last night would never happen again. So much for promises of sex tonight. She was much more concerned that what they'd experienced might never be on the table again.

CHAPTER 15

Two weeks later...

"They're going to be here soon," Dade said from the table without looking up.

"I know." She was watching out the window, excited for visitors. Ryan had come last week to bring them supplies and take another blood sample. Emily had come with him, which was a wonderful treat since Blair missed having a woman around to talk to.

The bloodwork had shown little change, which was good news. The disease was progressing slowly. Ryan had tossed out several options from blood transfusions to medicines to treat the symptoms to going forward with the cure for AP12 and taking them to the next phase.

Dade still hedged. She couldn't blame him. She wasn't sure which direction he should take either.

He had remained distant from her this entire time, and though she hated it, she respected his decision to pull back and keep her at arm's length. He had a lot on his mind. She couldn't imagine what he was feeling or thinking. If the roles were reversed, she wasn't sure she would react differently.

She was certain sex would be the last thing on his mind, however, so she never brought it up. Instead, she took what he gave her and held him tight when he let her.

At night, he slept in her bed, wrapped against her as if drawing from her strength silently. She would give him anything he needed. Though it weighed on her heavily, she never said a word. She didn't want to push him, physically or emotionally, so she gave him what he seemed to need and didn't pressure him for more.

When the truck pulled up, she jumped to her feet and headed for the door. Luckily, the weather had cooperated again today. Snow had fallen over the weekend, but it was clearer now, and the roads were passable.

She wasn't sure who was coming this morning, but she was surprised to see a man she didn't know stepping out of the back of the truck. He looked very tired. In fact, he struggled to take a single step.

"Fuck me," Dade murmured from her side as he whipped open the front door and ran past her toward the vehicle.

She watched as his face lit up while he and Ryan flanked the weak man to help him into the cabin. A light bulb went off, and she knew this was Zeke. He had only been awake ten days. He would still be tired and weak. He would not be infected with AP12 because he got the treatment as soon as he was reanimated.

Blair was shocked that Ryan would bring another person into the fold, exposing their location. But as she watched the way Dade's expression lit up, she realized the two of them had been very close friends. Ryan knew what he was doing. Maybe he intended to lift Dade's spirits with the visit.

Zeke was about six feet tall, four inches shorter than Dade, with brown wavy hair and deep green eyes she could see even from a distance.

Blair stood back and held the door open to let the trio inside.

Zeke met her gaze as he took deep breaths. "You must be Blair." He held out a hand.

"You must be Zeke." She shook his hand, surprised by his firm grip even in his state of weakness.

He didn't exactly smile, and she got the sense he rarely did. He met her gaze warmly, but it didn't extend beyond his eyes.

Dade kept a hand on his arm and led him to the couch where Zeke plopped down with a sigh as if he'd run a mile in under six minutes. "I'll be glad when I'm able to get around better," he told the room at large.

Dade sat next to him. "It won't take long. I came here at two weeks and progressed quickly. Of course, Blair has an amazing home gym."

Zeke shifted his gaze to her again as she leaned against the armchair, motioning Ryan to sit in it. "Your place is amazing and perfect. Thank you for harboring my friend."

"Of course." She smiled, finding she liked him in spite of his seriousness. "My pleasure."

A slight awkward silence followed, making her wonder if either of these two knew she was more than just a bodyguard or even a friend to Dade. They hadn't had sex again after that first night, but she still considered them to be something in between friends and a couple.

No way would she do anything to reveal that in front of the others, but she wondered how perceptive they were or if Dade had told Ryan anything.

Dade started asking Zeke questions. "Were you shocked when you first found out it had been ten years?"

Zeke nodded. "Stunned. It's still strange. There's this entire new team rushing around the bunker. They look just like we did a decade ago. Ants in an anthill on a mission. I find myself feeling like I'm out of body, watching them move, unable to do much else yet, and so far behind the times that my head spins."

Dade nodded. "That's a perfect description. How is everyone else? Kate? Grayson? Colton?"

Besides Zeke, three other people had been reanimated at the same time. They were the first group since three more chambers had been added to revive them.

"They're all good. Grayson is bossing everyone around. Colton only tells jokes. And Kate is quiet."

"Good to know their personalities are intact," Dade joked.

"Yep. How are you?" Zeke asked, sucking the air out of the room.

Dade sobered, shrugging. "Hanging in there."

Zeke must have known better than to bring up anemia, so he went another direction. "It was crazy riding out here in the back of that delivery truck."

"Yes. I was only a few days' further post-reanimation than you when we came here. I thought I was going to get tossed so hard against the side of the vehicle I would break a bone." Dade looked at Blair for the first time since everyone came in. "Luckily Blair was riding with me. She kept me from getting thrown from the back." His smile was warm as he held her gaze.

She didn't think he had looked at her for that many seconds in over a week. And he sure hadn't smiled often. Besides, his side of the story was a fabrication. She hadn't touched him during the drive. She'd worried he was too weak to hold on, but she hadn't reached for him out of fear for her life.

So far all he'd done at the time was grumble and complain. She hadn't known him well enough to be sure he wouldn't backhand her if she insulted his masculinity.

When Dade finally looked back at Zeke, the two of them joined Ryan in shop talk, discussing their research on several diseases.

Blair left them alone to go grab the groceries from the back of the truck. She restocked the fridge and set a few drinks on the coffee table next.

They continued talking for a long time, and then Ryan took a blood sample from Dade.

Blair was in the kitchen, pretending she belonged there and trying to look busy when she heard Ryan speaking. "Think about what I said. The choice is yours, but we need to make some decisions soon."

Dade nodded, not lifting his gaze.

Blair's heart rate picked up. She was always on edge lately, but they'd been living in a zone for the last few weeks. No, she didn't have all of Dade. She only had a fraction of him, and it was a distracted fraction. But it was better than nothing, and she'd learned to live with it. She would rather freeze time right where they were and have a quarter of the amazing man that was Dade Menke than have to give him up altogether.

The clock was ticking. Every time they had to make another decision, she flinched. She was scared out of her mind, both for herself and for Dade. And she hadn't spoken to a single person about her feelings. There wasn't any way to do so. It wasn't like she could call Emily or Temple and air her concerns. The cabin was too small for that kind of privacy. So, she sucked it up and pushed her emotions down deep, the burden growing by the day.

She couldn't even cry except in the shower for fear he would hear her. And the last thing she wanted to do was cause him undo stress. Though they slept in the same bed at night, and he usually tucked himself against her back, they were growing more estranged by the day. It hurt.

She also wasn't unaware that he was exhausted at night and slept longer. He never said a word, but she often saw him rubbing his temples when he was awake as though he had a constant headache.

She knew Dade and Ryan had been discussing his options at length, but had they decided on a path? And when would he tell her?

As Zeke and Ryan made their way to the door, Ryan spoke

again. "We'll get everything set up to bring Lawson Danforth here in a few days."

"Sounds good. Let me know if you need me to do anything from my end," Dade said.

Blair recognized the name. Danforth was the executor of Dade's grandfather's will. She hadn't realized Dade had plans to meet with the guy, but she was glad he was finally making something happen.

As Dade opened the front door, Blair came closer to say goodbye.

Zeke turned toward her. "Nice to meet you."

"You too. Don't worry. You'll get stronger every day, incrementally."

He nodded. "I hope so."

Ryan hugged Blair. "You okay?" he asked, holding her a few inches away, his eyes narrowed with concern.

"Of course," she lied, forcing a smile.

He drew his brows in farther. "I'll have Emily call you."

As she pulled back and glanced at Dade, she found him in a tight embrace with Zeke. She had to swallow over the lump in her throat as it became perfectly clear why Ryan had taken a chance and let Zeke in on Dade's location. Zeke had wanted to say goodbye to his friend.

"Sounds good." *It won't change anything, though.*

She stood next to Dade and watched them drive away. The air in the room was dense when they shut the door.

"So, Danforth is going to come?" she started.

"Sounds like it. I've exchanged a few emails with Ryan about it." He pointed at a folder on the coffee table she hadn't noticed. "Ryan brought me several things. Birth certificate. Social security card. The will."

"Oh, shit. I never thought about you needing identification."

"Temple has a way of getting things expedited. I'm the fourth person to reenter society after all. It's weird when someone has been declared dead to get them un-dead and get their status changed. If I hadn't needed the documents in order to collect whatever my grandfather left me, I would have told her not to bother."

Blair stiffened as Dade headed for the kitchen and started pulling out stuff for sandwiches. She detested when he spoke like that.

She followed him, choosing to ignore his fatalistic comments. "Zeke seems nice."

Dade chuckled. "No, he doesn't. No one describes Zeke as nice. Serious maybe. Surly even. But not nice."

"Well, he's not mean. I was just making small talk." She sounded sharp even to her own ears, but she was unable to hold back her frustration all of a sudden.

He dropped several things on the table and then paused to look up at her. "Are you mad about something?"

She shook her head. "No."

He sighed. "You're pissed."

"I'm not." She didn't want to fight with him, nor did she want him to have to stress over anything to do with her. Her job was to protect him, and part of that job had begun to include protecting him from himself and from her. If he wanted to keep stuff from her, she would let him. If he wanted to pout, she would let him. If he wanted to have a tantrum, she would let him.

More importantly, she wanted to be there for him to fill whatever need he had, emotional or maybe one day physical again because this wasn't about her. She didn't have a right to be pissed. He was the one dying. Not her.

He finished making the first sandwich and handed it to her. "I've been a bit of an ass lately. I'm sorry."

She took it from his fingers, leery about where this conversation might lead. "You haven't. You're preoccupied, and you have a right to be. You have a lot on your mind, and it's understandable. It would eat into your time to stop and explain things to me throughout the day. You don't owe me explanations. You have a job to do. And so do I. They don't exactly cross."

He perched on the stool across from her, but set his sandwich on the napkin. "Damn, I really am an ass."

She flinched. "Didn't I just say you were not?"

He laughed. "Your words maybe, but your tone indicated otherwise. I haven't been sharing anything with you. It was rude. Even if we meant nothing to each other besides roommates or client-slash-bodyguard, it would be insensitive to leave you out of the details."

She shrugged. There was an apology in there. She needed to take it. "I don't expect you to coddle me. I'm a grown-up. I understand."

He reached across the table and grabbed her hand. "I'm sorry."

"Okay." She tugged her hand free and pointed at his sandwich. "Eat. We must have some research we should be doing."

He shook his head, not meeting her gaze. "Not really."

"What do you mean?"

"I mean that we're out of options and time. I'm going to do the stem cell transplant."

She sat up straighter. "Seriously? When did you decide that?"

He exhaled slowly. "Kinda this morning. I mean, I've been thinking about it a lot. I need to act soon. My chances of success go down incrementally with every passing day that AP12 gets a stronger hold on me. The transplant has a much higher likelihood of working if I'm healthy at the time."

"But you've been working so hard to find another option, and you haven't had any symptoms. What about a bone marrow donor or even a cure?" She had no idea why she was arguing with him. It was stupid. She had believed all along he should take the stem cell transplant route.

Now that the decision was at hand, she was downright scared, though. What if it didn't work?

He lifted his head and met her gaze. "It'll be okay."

Would it?

No. It most certainly would not. Not if he died. It would never be okay. She'd lived a lifetime in the past few weeks. She couldn't imagine a life without him.

Her throat squeezed shut. The sandwich suddenly held no appeal. Her vision got blurry.

Shit. She didn't want him to see her emotional. She pushed from the table. "Excuse me." Attempting to remain calm, she headed to her bedroom and shut the door. She needed to be alone to pull her shit together. She didn't want him to see her like this.

She was supposed to be strong and indifferent. For him. For herself. For both of them.

She was failing.

CHAPTER 16

Dade cleaned up the kitchen, mostly to give Blair some time. He knew she had been emotional, on the edge of crying in fact. And she'd gracefully left the room to keep it from him. Unsuccessfully.

He also knew this was his fault. He'd held her at arm's length for two weeks. For his own self-preservation or hers? He didn't know anymore. But it had been stupid, and it had backfired.

He'd thought if he gently pushed her away, it would hurt less when he had to leave her for good. Hurt him less. Hurt her less.

She had plainly told him otherwise, but he hadn't listened. He'd been pigheaded and ignored her. He'd done a fine job of ignoring her ever since.

What he should have done was spent the last two weeks enjoying every moment with her. Also for both their sakes. Right? He wasn't sure he could repair the damage, but he sure as hell had to try.

Soon, he would leave her. She would never see him again. He had a plan. And it was time to implement it. In a few days he would sign the papers Danforth needed to get him his inheritance. He would also sign new papers that willed whatever money remained.

A few days after that he would get two injections, one to cure AP12 and the other to fill his blood with his own stem cells. And then he would disappear. He figured he had about a 40 percent chance of surviving. Those odds were not good, and he didn't want anyone he knew to walk through the end of life with him. So, he would leave. It would hurt Blair, but not as badly as watching him die. She'd already held her sister's dying body. He wouldn't add to those mental images with his own body.

But first, he needed to talk to her. Make her understand.

He wiped his hands on his jeans and headed for her bedroom. After knocking softly, he waited. It took her a few seconds before she said, "Come in."

At first he couldn't see her anywhere, so he stepped around to the far side of the bed, and there she was, sitting on the floor, her back against the mattress, her knees drawn to her chest. She was rocking forward and backward slightly, facing the floor.

Fuck.

He crouched near her to one side. "I'm sorry."

"I know. Don't worry. I just needed a few minutes alone."

"I gave you a few."

She said nothing.

He sighed. "I've botched everything."

She kept rocking.

"I thought it would be easier if I put some distance between us."

"I told you it wouldn't be. Not for me."

"I know. I didn't listen." He lowered to the floor, sitting on his ass. He wanted to reach out to her, hold her, stroke her hair. She didn't seem receptive to that.

"When is this Danforth guy coming?"

"In two days."

She nodded at the floor again. "So your plan is to sign his papers, collect your money, get the treatment shot for AP12,

147

follow that with the stem cell transplant, and then take off to die alone. Do I have that right?"

His breath caught. He'd hidden nothing from her. She was too smart.

Suddenly, she released her knees and lifted her face to glare at him. "Do I have that fucking right?"

He blinked, shocked by her outburst.

"At least have the balls to admit your plan to my face before you fucking leave in the middle of the night without telling anyone where you're going, you selfish asshole."

His mouth fell open to respond, but he wasn't sure what to say. This was the second time she'd called him that. *If the words fit...* She was right. He was selfish, but he was protecting himself as well as her.

She reached out and grabbed his shirt, tugging his chest forward so he was forced to face her. "You're a coward. You can tell yourself you're doing all this to save me from having to watch you die, but the truth is you're too scared to feel anything yourself. You're afraid to show vulnerability.

"You're afraid to admit you're fucking scared to death. You're afraid to cry in front of anyone, or scream, or stomp, or throw things. You're also afraid to live. Afraid to enjoy yourself because it will hurt more." She shoved him back and released his shirt.

He lifted his face as she pushed to standing.

She stared down at him, fury in her eyes. "Stop lying to everyone, especially me. This has very little to do with me. You can tell yourself you're doing all this to spare me or Ryan or Tushar or Trish or Temple or Zeke from having to watch you die, but you're fucking lying. You're doing it because you're afraid to feel anything for anyone because it will hurt *you*.

"You're right. It will be so much easier to drive away from here, cut all ties, and find some out-of-the-way hotel on the beach to spend your last days. You can sit and watch the sunset all by yourself, and no one will see you cry or have to watch you suffer. It will be easier, but you're going to be the loneliest bastard on the planet lying in some hotel room martyring yourself for humanity." She stomped around him and left the room.

He was still sitting there, too stunned to move, when he heard the back door open and slam shut. He flinched, but he still didn't move. He couldn't. Her words hurt him, but she was totally right. He was indeed a world-class selfish asshole who was afraid to let the best thing that had ever happened to him get close enough to love.

He'd done this himself. She'd been nothing but patient while he spent day after day acting like an idiot. She'd honored his wishes and let him wallow in self-pity, and now she'd had enough. Rightfully so.

The question was how was he going to fix this? Was it too late?

He shoved to his feet and took a deep breath. He would go after her and grovel at her feet if it was the last thing he did.

Because it turned out there was something worse than hurting her by letting her watch him die. He just hadn't let himself recognize it. Pushing her away until she was bitter and angry with him and seeing that on her face and how badly he'd hurt her with his actions was far worse.

Yep. He was a dick. And he headed for the back door to chase her down and do his best to right this wrong. Based on the rhythmic sound of her axe, he wouldn't have to go far. He just hoped she didn't cut a finger off in her anger.

Dade didn't even bother to grab his coat on his way outside. Neither had Blair. She was wearing just as much clothing as him —jeans, boots, a long-sleeved thermal shirt. Her hair was pulled back in her usual ponytail. And she was chopping the wood in front of her into tiny shards that could now be used as kindling, or perhaps toothpicks if he gave her much more time.

It was dangerous, however, for her to continue in her current state of mind. So, he rushed across the yard and wrapped his arms around her middle, grabbing her axe-wielding wrist with one hand.

She struggled against him, elbowing his stomach and shoving him with her shoulders.

He didn't let go. In fact, he held her tighter, seriously concerned about the damn hatchet she still held. He shook her wrist. "Drop the axe, Blair."

She fought him for several more seconds until he set his lips on her ear and whispered, "Drop the axe, baby. Please." Finally, she released it. The second it hit the ground, she let out a piercing cry that reached his soul.

He pulled her tighter, her back against his front, him now holding her arms to her sides to keep her from hurting either of them.

After long seconds, she went limp, sobbing, muttering unintelligibly.

"It's okay. I've got you." He rocked her, trying to soothe her enough to get her back inside. It was fucking cold out.

As if all the energy drained from her body, her legs gave out.

Dade nearly dropped her. She almost slid between his arms to the ground. But he caught her, lifted her into his arms, and carried her back inside.

Shocking him further, she seemed to recover enough of herself when he shut the door to squirm free of him. "Put me down," she shouted, furious. She pushed against him, causing him to nearly drop her again as she fought to free herself.

He set her on her feet before they both fell, and she scrambled backward. Her gorgeous blue eyes were dark and angry when she growled, "Don't you have a suitcase to pack or something? Or better yet, why bother? You're just going to die anyway. No reason to waste clothes. Just go in whatever you're wearing. Who cares if you change? You'll be alone anyway."

He swallowed, wishing she would calm down enough for him

to try to apologize again. He'd done this. He'd brought this on himself.

She kept rambling—her way of getting all her frustration out of her system. Interrupting her seemed like a bad idea. "I think I have a computer bag around here somewhere. You could take the laptop so you can play some video games or watch movies while you wait to die."

He gripped the back of one of the kitchen chairs, holding his tongue.

She backed up and yanked open the pantry. "We're all stocked with new snacks. You want me to pack your favorites so you'll have nice things to eat in the hotel room?" She reached inside, grabbed a box of Cheez-Its, and threw them on the counter. "How about peanut butter granola bars? I know you like those." They joined the Cheez-Its. "Oh, and Chex mix. You'll need some of that." The box hit the granola bars and fell on the floor.

Dade inched closer, unsure what to do while she was so unhinged.

She slammed the pantry closed and held out her hands. "Stop. Don't touch me. Don't you ever touch me."

"Blair…" She was killing him.

She kept backing up until she was in the living room. "You win. I give up. Go. Slink off by yourself to die. Maybe if you don't die, you can send a postcard letting us all know. Or better yet, take a new identity and disappear. It will hurt less than keeping in touch with the people who love you."

The lump in his throat made it difficult to speak. "Blair, stop. Please." He followed her, but kept several feet between them.

"*No,*" she screamed. She stomped her foot. "No. Don't tell me what to do or feel or think. I'm done letting you dictate how things are. I've had enough of pretending it doesn't matter and letting you run the show.

"I'm falling in love with you, you idiot. And you've trampled over me for weeks." Tears ran down her face, and she didn't bother to wipe them away. "It hurts. You thought you could push me away to spare my feelings. Well, it didn't work. I fell for you anyway. And you don't get it. You don't get that I'd rather hold you and care about you and love you through this entire thing."

She sobbed, trying to catch her breath, and then continued. "We don't always pick who we love or what we're going to do about it. I fell for you, and you tossed it aside to keep from dealing with any emotions. Obviously you don't feel the same as me. I get that."

"I do, Blair." The words came out rapidly.

Her body jerked. Her eyes went wide. And then she shook her head. "No. You don't. Because if you did, you would understand that I don't care if you're dying. I still want to be with you. Will it hurt? Hell, yes. But walking away would hurt more. If the treatment doesn't work and you get sick, I want to hold you in my arms and comfort you. The fact that you can't get that speaks volumes." She turned around and headed for her bedroom, her shoulders falling.

He followed her, rushing forward. Just as she stepped through the doorframe, he wrapped his arms around her from behind and pulled her close.

She didn't fight him, surprisingly, though he assumed it was because she was drained. "Let me go," she whispered. "I'll sleep in the guest bedroom."

"No, you won't. You'll listen to me as I stumble over trying to explain myself."

"There's nothing left to say." Her arms hung at her sides, and her head was tipped forward.

"There's a lot to say. You got to speak your mind; now let me speak mine." When she didn't object again, he found the will to continue. "I love you, Blair. So much it hurts. So much that I lie awake at night holding you in my arms wishing I could have more. So much that I find myself watching you move around the cabin instead of focusing on my computer half the time. I love you, baby."

She let out a sob.

"You're right. About everything. Maybe your next job can be as a psychiatrist, because you're always right when you analyze me. I was wrong. All my thoughts were stupid. I wasted two weeks of what could have been special between us because I've been stubborn and idiotic. I'm so sorry." He loosened his grip, spun her around, and smoothed a hand up her arm until he could brush her hair back from her face.

She leaned her head on his chest. Silent tears were still falling.

He swung her up in his arms again and carried her across the room to sit her on the bed. After grabbing a pile of tissues from the nightstand, he handed them to her.

She wiped her face and blew her nose. Finally, she lifted her gaze to him. Her eyes were swollen and puffy. "You're not just saying all that?"

"No." He shook his head and then cupped her face, tipping it back as he stepped closer to her, crowding her. He leaned down and kissed her gently. "No. I mean every word. I love you."

"I love you too," she whispered against his mouth. "Can you stop acting like an idiot?"

He smiled. "Yes. I promise. I'm so sorry. I won't push you away again. I'll share everything I know and what I'm planning." He kissed her again, deepening the contact this time, grateful when her hands went around his waist and held him closer.

He tangled his fingers in her hair, releasing the band that held it back so that the thick blond locks fell loose down her back. He ran his hands through it over and over while he kissed her. It was so soft, and it soothed him to stroke through the length.

When she moaned into his mouth and lowered her hands to grip his butt, he instantly got hard. He'd denied himself for so long that an urgency overtook him, making him crave more.

As her fingers made their way under his shirt, he reached for the hem of hers and drew it over her head. While she was still tugging on his sleeves, he cupped her breasts.

She shoved him, causing him to lose his balance as he took a step backward. The kiss broke. Confused, he met her gaze.

But her mission was immediately obvious as she reached for the button on her jeans and nodded toward his. "Clothes off. Now."

He smirked at her bossiness while he obeyed. When they were both completely naked, he stalked toward her.

She backed up, crawling across the bed.

He climbed over her, hovering above her body, staring down at her, thanking his lucky stars. Damn, she was beautiful.

In another stunning move, she grabbed his shoulders and flipped him onto his back. Two seconds later, she was straddling him on her knees, her hands flat on his chest, her warmth against the edge of his erection.

He moaned.

She smiled. "Maybe I *can* be bossy in bed." When she lifted, his length throbbed against her, and then she lined her channel up with him and lowered herself down until she was fully seated.

His vision swam as all his blood rushed unexpectedly to his torso. When she lifted off and slammed back down, he lost his breath. His hand somehow made it to her waist, but she controlled the pace she set and the intensity. The entire time, she held his gaze, hers smoldering.

Dade was so hard, it was a wonder he didn't come instantly. A miracle, really, since she showed no mercy. She rode him at an excruciatingly slow speed, using her incredible leg strength to ease on and off him effortlessly.

He watched her face, noticing every emotion as she enjoyed herself. When she slid one hand down to touch her clit, he lost it. He needed to change the direction of this show before he totally lost control.

He gripped her hips and flipped her onto her back so fast, she was stunned. The connection was broken in the movement, but he spread her legs wide, lined up with her wet heat, and thrust into her before she could protest.

Apparently she didn't mind the change because a soft moan escaped her lips and her eyes fluttered shut.

He slid his knees forward, lifting her hips off the bed, and remained inside her while he tucked a pillow under her ass.

Her fingers grabbed at the sheets while her wild gaze found his. Her mouth hung open, but she didn't speak. Good. He hoped he'd rendered her speechless. And the gap between her lips widened when he found her clit with his fingers and flicked the swollen nub rapidly.

Instead of pumping in and out of her, he watched her face as she climbed to the edge. He kept playing with her clit, rubbing and circling and flicking the tip until she cried out, gritting her teeth, her entire body stiffening with her orgasm. He didn't stop until her butt relaxed between his knees.

And then he grabbed her thighs, drew himself out, and thrust back in. Heaven.

She was soft and hard at the same time, pliant from just coming, but she also set her hands on top of his and gripped them for dear life, silently asking for more.

He gave her more. He gave both of them more. Thrusting faster and harder while he gritted his own teeth until he finally came, buried inside her. The happiest man alive.

Arms shaking, he slid out of her before he would have liked and eased onto his side, drawing her close.

She turned toward him, wrapping her arm around his middle and holding him tight. "You okay?" she asked, tipping her face back to meet his eyes.

He nodded.

"You're shaking." She rubbed her hand up and down his arm.

"I'm fine."

She looked extremely worried.

He kissed her lips, trying to control his tremor. "Baby, I'm fine. This is not a symptom of some stupid form of anemia. I'm just overwhelmed with emotion. I just made love to the woman I'm so in love with she takes my breath away."

A slow smile spread across her lips, and she tucked her head against his shoulder and squeezed him as close as possible.

Yeah, he was a lucky son of a bitch.

CHAPTER 17

"So, where do you need him to sign, Mr. Danforth?" Blair asked.

"Please, call me Lawson." Lawson Danforth turned out to be significantly younger than she expected. He was probably in his early thirties. Five ten. Lanky. Dark hair and skin. A full suit. He was very professional. He'd arrived fifteen minutes ago with Ryan and Tushar, and so far he'd spent most of that time staring at Dade.

Dade stood on the front porch. He couldn't get any closer to Lawson without the risk of infecting the man with AP12. It wasn't completely irresponsible because there was a cure for AP12, but Lawson hadn't been immunized, and there was no sense taking a chance he might be exposed.

He was also a notary, which made things much smoother because the more people who came out to the cabin, the more danger Dade would be in. Keeping the number of folks who knew he existed and where he was located a secret was still a top priority.

"Right here and right here," Lawson said, pointing at a spot on two different pieces of official-looking paper he held on top of a thick bound folder. He glanced at Ryan. "This is the most unconventional meeting I've ever had with a client."

Ryan nodded. "And I can't express to you vehemently enough how important it is for you to keep this to yourself. The only reason we ever contacted you and agreed to this farce was so that Dade could enjoy whatever money his grandfather left him. We spent weeks debating the merits of arranging this meeting."

"And you say he's contagious with the same viral anemia that caused him to be frozen for ten years in the first place?" Lawson looked skeptical.

Blair let Ryan handle this conversation, waiting patiently next to the men for Lawson to pass her the papers.

Ryan nodded. "Not frozen exactly. It's called vitrification. But yes. It's complicated. He hasn't been able to get the treatment."

"I see." Clearly the man didn't see anything. His gaze shot back to Dade. "The circumstances are extraordinary, but I can't think of a single legal reason why we would need to be standing closer than this for your signature to be acceptable. I can see you signing just fine. I have all the proof I need to assure me you are indeed Dade Menke. So, I guess this is it." He handed the papers and folder to Blair. "I just need the signed pages. Dade keeps the will."

She carried them to Dade, gave him a pen, and waited while he signed where she indicated.

As she returned to Lawson, he spoke to Dade again. "The funds will be transferred to the account Ryan set up for you. I trust you're aware of all this and have agreed to the arrangements. I can have the money deposited tomorrow. It won't be difficult."

Dade leaned against the post at the top of the steps. "And you signed a NDA, correct?"

Lawson nodded. "Yes. I assure you no one will find out about you from me. I'm a professional. I wouldn't be in this job if people couldn't trust me. I've kept some weird secrets. Yours might be one of the strangest, but word of your existence won't leak from me."

"We appreciate you coming all the way out here, Mr. Danforth," Tushar added. "I know it was unconventional."

"No problem. I'm just glad I could help fulfill Mr. Menke's dying wishes. The older Mr. Menke," he rushed to add. "When he first came to me with this crazy plan of his, I thought he'd lost his mind. But he must have had foresight, because he was right."

Dade cleared his throat. "Just out of curiosity, how much money are we talking about? I assume it's got to be significant enough for you to go to so much trouble to find me, but you've never indicated exactly how much."

Lawson smiled as he handed Blair a sealed envelope. "I don't think you'll be disappointed. Please accept my sorrow on the death of your grandfather. I didn't know him well, and it's been a few years, but I know it's fresh news to you. He was a good man. He probably should have enjoyed his life a bit more and saved a bit less, but I think he truly believed you would need the money more than he ever did. So he left it. And his gamble paid off."

"Thank you for everything," Tushar stated. "We can take you back to your car now if you're ready."

"Of course." Lawson nodded toward Dade. "Have a nice day."

Blair was confused by the look on Lawson's face and the strange little speech. She wondered if Dade had been able to see his odd expressions from so far away. Envelope in hand, she returned to the porch as Ryan, Tushar, and Lawson got back in the car. She stood by Dade's side, waving as they pulled away.

When they were gone, she handed him the envelope. "You think it'll be enough to get us to Hawaii or someplace at least warm and sunny?" She was half joking. It would take several thousand dollars in airfare alone to make a trip like that.

She had some money stashed away, and she would contribute whatever was necessary to get Dade someplace pleasant, but there was no way to know how long they would be there once they arrived, and they couldn't live forever off her meager savings.

She planned to take a leave of absence from her job. After

several conversations with Temple, they had agreed that as soon as Dade received the treatment, if he wanted to disappear and go somewhere unspecified, he was on his own. The government couldn't provide him protection if he essentially went rogue. Which meant they would no longer be assigning Blair to his detail.

Which also meant Blair would take time off to accompany him. She wasn't prepared to think beyond that plan. What ifs made her queasy, so she was noncommittal about how long she would be gone and when she might come back to the bunker and even *if* she would return. Temple guaranteed her three months' unpaid leave without risk to her position. After that, they would need to renegotiate.

Dade threaded his fingers with hers and led her into the house. "It's cold out here." He shut the door and shrugged out of his coat, hanging it on a hook by the front door. "Shall we see if we're going to need a bus ticket or if we can afford a plane?" he joked, tapping the envelope he held in his free hand.

She followed him to the couch and sat next to him, her curiosity piqued.

He set the thick folder with the will on his knees and opened the envelope casually to pull out one piece of trifolded paper. Letterhead. Simple. One sentence. A signature. And a number that made her lean closer.

"Holy shit," Dade murmured.

"Wow." She glanced up. "You want me to hire a private jet or just buy the airline?"

His eyes were wide with shock. "Who knew my grandfather was so frugal?" He set the letter on the coffee table and opened the will. "Surely there's a logical explanation."

"Yeah, but it might take you a month to read all that."

He flipped through the pages, pausing every once in a while, until he finally reached the end and closed it. "Looks like he bought some bonds years ago and then later invested in very lucrative stocks. He got lucky, and then he held on to the proceeds."

"I'd say you're the one who got lucky."

He dropped the folder on the coffee table with the letter, smiled at her as he stroked her chin, and then melted her heart with his words. "I definitely got lucky, but it had nothing to do with that will." His lips descended while her heart picked up the pace.

Two hours later they were lying in her bed, neither of them having spoken for several minutes while they caught their breath. She snuggled into Dade's side, one leg wrapped over his thigh, her hand on his chest, her cheek against his pecs. "So, what's the plan?" she asked.

"You mean for lunch or the next few months?"

She giggled. "Well, both."

"As for lunch, I suggest you shower while I make us something to eat because I'm starving, and I don't want to have to pretend to enjoy burnt sandwiches."

She swatted his chest. "I've never burned the sandwiches. I don't even cook them."

He chuckled low and deep, the sound vibrating against her cheek and making her content. When he was finished, he continued. "As for the extended plan, Ryan and I bumped heads earlier."

"I figured that's what you were doing while I met with Tushar and Lawson by the car."

Dade started a leisurely stroke up and down her arm. "Yes. So, we agreed on a few things. Only two people are going to know what's going on—Tushar and Ryan."

She lifted her head. "Not even Emily, Trish, or Temple?"

Temple was in charge of the entire project. How could they keep her out of the loop?

He shook his head. "Nope. Just the two of them. We don't want to take the risk of a single human knowing where I am. The fewer people involved, the better."

"Okay." If he cut her out of this equation, she would absolutely lose her shit. "Keep going."

"Ryan is going to come on Monday. He's going to give me the cure for AP12 and then follow that immediately with the stem cell treatment. After he leaves, we're going to take the Jeep and head west. We can look at a map and plan the details together."

At least he hadn't insinuated even for a second that she wasn't included. Thank God they were past that. "An adventure."

"Yep. I thought we could meander toward the ocean at first and then pick a spot at our whim."

"You mean you don't want to hop a plane to Jamaica or Hawaii?" she teased.

"We can do that later. But let's get a few weeks under our belt first." Code for *wait and see if the stem cell transplant is working.*

She nodded. "Sounds good. So we need to pack our things and be prepared to leave in a few days."

"Is that okay?" he asked, still stroking her arm.

"Yes. Of course."

He slid his hand up her arm and lifted her face to meet her gaze. "You don't have to do this, you know."

She groaned. "Dade…"

"I know. I know. You're tired of me bringing this up. This is the last time I'm going to mention it. You have other options. You could go back to the bunker Monday and go on with your life, for example. I'll be fine."

She glared at him.

"Or you can go with me and hold my hand while I silently freak out with worry every day, waiting to see if the stem cells do their job."

"That's the only option."

He pulled her chin closer. "I love you."

She smiled, emotion bubbling up from inside again. Overflowing. "I love you too. We're in this together. For better or for worse. I'm not leaving you, so don't mention it again."

"Deal."

She needed to move away from him before she started crying. The last thing she wanted was for him to have to watch her cry all the time. She would have to figure out a way to keep it tamped down, especially if he got sick. It would be hard, but she would do it. "I'm going to take a shower now," she whispered. "Fix me something to eat. I'm hungry."

"Yes, boss. I'm on it."

As she padded to the bathroom, she glanced back over her shoulder to find Dade propped up on an elbow, watching her. She paused, capturing the moment in her mind. He looked happy, his lips curled slightly in a smile, his eyes filled with emotion. His hair was a rumpled mess, and his chest was broad and defined.

He looked like a man who just had the most satisfying sex. Hopefully, he felt that way too.

Yeah, this was going to be hard, but she wouldn't have it any other way.

CHAPTER 18

On Monday morning, their bags were packed and loaded in the Jeep before Ryan pulled up to the cabin. He had a surprising number of items in his hands as he came inside.

"What's all this?" Blair asked as he set everything on the kitchen table.

"I'll explain."

Dade set his hands on the back of a chair and perused Ryan's assortment also. He reached for a hard-sided, gray case that looked like the cross between a small suitcase and a briefcase. "Please tell me this is what I think it is."

Blair imagined it containing weapons or some important secret government documents.

Ryan nodded. "If you think it's a portable blood tester, then you're right."

"Awesome." Dade popped the latches on the case and opened it to reveal a variety of lab equipment Blair couldn't identify if her life depended on it. Except it was possible Dade's life might very well depend on it, and she would need to know how to use it eventually. She had wondered how they would know if the stem cell transplant was working.

"A group at Caltech invented it a few years ago. It's amazing."

Dade was grinning like a kid with a new toy train—a scientist's version of a cool gadget.

Ryan had also brought in several other bags which he proceeded to open. When he unfolded a kit that looked like it was intended for surgery, she winced. "What's all that?" She sure didn't want to find out she would need to use *it* at some point. A blood draw and testing equipment she could handle. A scalpel —never.

Ryan ignored Blair and looked at Dade. "I'm going to swap the tracker out."

Dade swallowed and slid into the chair. "Swap it?"

Ryan nodded. "Too many people know about it. You might as well be a green dot moving around the country. But I'd still like to be able to find you if needed, and reaching you by phone won't be easy, so I'm going to put a new one in. I'll be the only person who knows about it."

Blair's spine tingled. This sounded serious. "How big is this tracker?" She winced.

Ryan glanced at her. "It's no big deal. It's much smaller than you would think."

Blair lowered herself onto a chair across from Dade, partially because her legs were shaking. She wasn't ordinarily a queasy sort of person, and she acknowledged she would probably need to get over any aversion to needles ASAP, but Ryan was holding a knife in his hand.

She shuddered to imagine a world where someone in the government or inside the bunker would actually hunt Dade down and kidnap him or worse. Even though her job had been to protect him from exactly that for all this time, it still seemed inconceivable.

Dade reached across the table and grabbed her hand, giving it a squeeze. Her fingers were cold, a fact she only noticed because his hand was so warm. She missed his touch immediately when he drew his hand back. His gaze was on Ryan. "Did something else happen?"

Ryan sighed. "Someone leaked details about the next four members of the team already, and they aren't even going to be fully awake for two more weeks. Extensive details. Their families. Their previous addresses. Everything."

"Damn." Ryan flinched. "You must be pulling your hair out."

"I am." Ryan faced Blair again. "It's only a small incision. Not a big deal. But if you don't want to watch, you could go in the other room."

Blair glanced at Dade's arm. "I'll be fine." At least she hoped so.

Ryan set Dade's wrist on a small towel, cleaned the spot with an antiseptic, and then used the tip of a cotton swab to apply something else.

"It'll numb the area a bit." He didn't wait long before he picked up a small scalpel and then gripped Dade's arm tightly to keep him from flinching while he made a little incision.

Surprisingly, Blair didn't look away. She was intrigued.

Dade winced, but otherwise remained still.

Ryan set the knife down and picked up some tweezers. "Might sting a bit. Hold tight." He squeezed Dade's arm, stuck the tweezers into the tiny cut, and miraculously pulled out the smallest silver square imaginable. "Got it." He was pleased with himself.

Blair was shaking her head. "That tiny thing is a GPS tracker?"

"Yep." He set it on the towel and then picked up a matching square she hadn't even seen with the tweezers and tucked it into the incision. Holding the small cut closed with one hand, he put a butterfly bandage over it and then grabbed a piece of gauze and pressed it against the wound.

Dade cleared his throat. "How many people know you just did that?"

"Three." Ryan dropped the first tracker in a baggy and sealed it shut.

Dade nodded. "Let me guess—Temple, Tushar, and Trish?"

"Nope."

Blair flinched as she realized the correct answer. "Dade, Ryan, and Blair." She spoke of the three of them as if they were not the people in the room.

Ryan nodded. "She's quick." He handed the baggy to Blair. "Put this in your pocket, guard it with your life, and leave it at the first motel. I made you a reservation." He handed her a piece of paper. Scrawled across the top was the information for the motel. "It's in your name. Check in. Go to the room. Hide this chip under the bed. Bury it in the carpet where a vacuum cleaner can't reach. Then leave."

Dade leaned back in the chair, releasing the pressure on his arm. "You're serious."

Ryan nodded. "I trust absolutely no one. I don't know who the fuck is finding you guys or how they're doing it, but this is now a dead end. If anyone ever finds you, then you'll know I personally had to be the mole."

"What about your dad? Surely you've spoken to Tushar."

Ryan shook his head. "We talked. We agreed I would make the arrangements and not even tell him. At first I worried what would happen if anything happened to me, but then we decided it didn't matter. The two of you know how to get in touch with anyone at the bunker at any time. You don't need someone on the inside with the specifics. After you leave that motel, even I won't know where you are. I'll only activate that new tracker if it becomes necessary for me to find you."

Ryan dug around in another bag and pulled out a throw-away phone. "I got you this to start with. They're inexpensive these days. I'd advise you not use it unless it's an emergency. Memorize my number, the bunker, Temple's, Tushar's. Don't program anything. If you need to call me, throw the phone away after and get another one." He handed them a list of numbers. "You know my regular number. I added a new one for a phone no one knows

I have. As long as I can keep that one a secret, we'll be able to use it."

Dade stared at the list and then looked up again. "You won't be able to reach us, then."

Ryan nodded.

Blair realized that was why Ryan had put the new tracker in. He would never have a phone number for them, but he could find them anyway if there were an emergency. Hell, he could easily locate them with enough accuracy to know what hotel they were staying in and call the front desk.

Dade inhaled long and slow. "So let me get this straight. We're going to leave here in the Jeep and drive to this motel and plant the tracker. You're thinking people will watch our location for a few days and assume we stayed at that motel to wait and see which way my health turns."

It wasn't a question. Blair realized Dade was simply spelling it all out.

Dade continued. "And the Jeep?"

"Leave it at the motel. I'll send someone to get it later."

Blair had so many questions, she didn't know where to begin. "How are we going to get another car? Won't anyone be able to track us by tracing our credit cards?"

Ryan pulled out a thick folder from another bag and slid it across the table.

When she opened it, she gasped. Driver's licenses. Passports. Credit cards. Everything John and Stacey Jones could possibly need for their trip. Her hands were shaking. "Jesus."

Dade leaned closer. "John and Stacey Jones?" He chuckled. "How original."

"How popular," Ryan pointed out. "Do you know how many people have those names in the US alone?"

"I can imagine," Dade responded. "And the money? I assume you transferred it to John's account?"

"Yep." Ryan reached across and pulled a sheet of paper from

farther down the pile. Bank account information. A joint account in the name of John and Stacey. "I suggest you look into bitcoin and set up an account. It will make it easier for you to make purchases without being tracked."

"What the hell is bitcoin?" Dade asked.

Blair nodded, trying not to freak out. "I have a basic idea. We'll figure it out. But jeez, this is serious." She met Ryan's gaze. "Why? I thought we were just going on a little vacation. How could anyone possibly care where we are or who we are?"

Ryan shrugged. "You have to ask that question? You were there when Emily got kidnapped. You got shot, for heaven's sake. And then my parents. We hid them on a ranch in Montana. So few people knew about that it was crazy. And yet, people tracked them down. They could have been killed."

Blair knew all that. She shouldn't find any of these plans to be excessive or unreasonable. She simply hadn't thought it through entirely. She should have. She was a freaking bodyguard. *Dade's* bodyguard. But somehow she'd gotten so wrapped up in her personal feelings for the man she was supposed to be guarding that she lost sight of the big picture. She felt like a fool. "You're right." She sighed.

Everyone was silent for a few moments.

Finally, she spoke again, her mind clearer, more focused on the safety aspects of this adventure. "You're leaving out some details."

Ryan nodded. "After you leave the hotel, you're on your own. Do whatever you want to do. Pick someplace safe to lay low. Move if the hair stands up on the back of your necks. Don't call in until it's necessary."

Dade studied or pretended to study the contents of the folder.

Blair knew what Ryan was saying. And one look from Ryan told her they were on the same page. There was more to this plan. Two paths—the one in which Dade lived and the one in which he did not. It would be up to Blair to communicate with Ryan and let him know which route they were on when they knew for sure.

She shuddered.

His eyes searched hers again until she nodded. What he didn't say was *call me when you know*, but she heard him loud and clear.

Ryan opened another bag and pulled out several more items. Among those items was a syringe like someone would use for an immunization and an IV bag filled with a milky substance that had to be the stem cells. "Ready?" he asked Dade.

Dade closed the folder and passed it to Blair. "Ready as I'll ever be, I guess. Where do you want to stick me?" His voice was light as he attempted to joke.

Ryan swabbed Dade's biceps and quickly injected him with the cure for AP12 that could also kill him.

Blair held her breath, her mouth dry as she watched the clear substance created to heal...and inadvertently harm. She hated that stupid shot and what it stood for.

"I'd rather you lie down for the stem cells," Ryan said. "It will take a while. About an hour."

Dade nodded and stood. Without a word, he headed for the master bedroom.

Blair followed and began fussing around, propping him up with pillows because she didn't know what else to do.

Ryan said nothing as he put an IV into Dade's arm and then attached the small bag of stem cells. This substance wasn't as ominous as the shot. Stem cells could do no harm. The question was how powerful were they, and could they save his life?

After attaching the bag to the headboard to keep it above Dade's body, Ryan put everything away. He looked down at Dade and touched his arm. "Good luck, man. We'll all be rooting for you. I'm sorry we didn't have better odds to work with. It wasn't for lack of trying."

"I know," Dade whispered. He reached with his free hand and grabbed Ryan's wrist. "Thank you. For everything. You did your best. The rest is out of our hands."

Ryan turned away and left the room without another word.

Blair leaned over and kissed Dade on the forehead. "I'll be right back." She followed Ryan to the kitchen. "I assume Dade will know what to do with that?" She pointed at the gray case.

"Yes. And there are instructions. Don't worry about it for a few days. I put a chart in there telling you when to test and what to look for. Wait forty-eight hours before you do it the first time. But you won't know anything from that first test. It will just give you a baseline. Two days later you can repeat the test and compare the results. And so on."

"It's not rocket science, is it? Either the blood cells are increasing or they're decreasing." She didn't know if they were looking at white or red or what, but it didn't matter. She understood the gist.

"Exactly."

Blair walked him outside to the car. Emotions welled up in her throat. She had no idea when or if she would ever see Ryan or anyone else again. She wasn't sure what to say. "My apartment… This cabin? My things?"

"I'll handle it. Emily will help me. No one is going to touch anything for the time being."

She nodded. Ryan had thought of everything. "I may never return."

"I know." He pursed his lips, clearly fighting the same emotions she was experiencing.

"Tell Emily how much I appreciated her friendship these last few months."

"I will. She knows."

Blair leaned her forehead against Ryan's chest and as he pulled her in for a hug. He didn't say it would be okay. It might never be okay. There were no guarantees. When she lifted her face again, he searched her eyes. "You clear on everything?"

"Yes. I can handle it. Use cash. Buy a car. Leave the Jeep. I've got it." She was rambling through the obvious parts.

"You'll call me on the burner phone."

"Yes." *When I know... When my life takes a sharp turn for the better or the worse.*

"There's more to say."

"I know that too." He had a plan for after. After they knew.

He reached into his pocket and pulled out an envelope, handing it to her. "These are some instructions for later. You can decide if you want to keep them to yourself or share them with Dade. You know him better than anyone. You'll know...what he can handle or wants to hear."

She nodded, swallowing back emotion.

"You're in love with him."

A tear escaped her eye. She pulled her lips between her teeth and bit down, nodding.

"He's a lucky guy."

I'm the lucky one. A few weeks with Dade was worth more than anything in the world. She would never regret this as long as she lived.

Ryan tucked a loose tendril of her hair behind her ear and hugged her again. And then he climbed into his car and drove away.

For a long time, Blair stood there, hugging herself, listening to the sounds of nature. She closed her eyes and took deep breaths. When she had her emotions under control, she headed back inside to see about the IV and load the last of their things into the Jeep.

CHAPTER 19

It was late afternoon when Blair pulled up to the motel Ryan had reserved under her name. She went to the desk, checked in, and asked that she not be disturbed for a few days because she wasn't feeling well and needed to rest. The manager made a note of it and assured her the housekeeping staff would skip that room.

Ryan had prepaid for three days. The man had left out no detail.

She parked her Jeep around back at the entrance to the room, went inside, and planted the chip deep in the carpet under the bed. By the time she came back outside, Dade was pulling up in the black Explorer they'd purchased an hour ago from a used lot. Cash.

She climbed into the passenger seat. "You want me to drive?"

"No. I'm fine." He leaned over and kissed her briefly before putting the SUV in drive and leaving the parking lot. "Where should we go?"

It seemed like now was a good time to shake off the somber mood and enjoy themselves, so she shot him a smile. "I don't know. Vegas?" she joked.

He laughed. "How fast do you think we could gamble away all that money?"

"I've never actually gambled. Nor have I been to Vegas."

"Really?" He glanced at her.

"Nope. But I was kidding. I'm not in the mood for the flashing lights and noise. How about someplace quiet. Peaceful."

"So back to your cabin?" he teased.

She sighed. "That would be nice."

"Okay. How about a national park in Utah? There are several. I bet it's beautiful there this time of year."

She reached across and took his hand. "I love that idea. You sure you want to drive?" He hadn't driven in ten years technically.

"It's like riding a bike. I'm fine. Besides, Ryan got me a license. I'm even legal." He patted his pocket.

"Great..." she drawled out, not impressed.

After spending the night in a hotel near the border of Utah and Colorado, they continued on the next morning. By afternoon they had rented a cabin for two weeks in Fishlake National Forest.

Dade was exhausted. It had nothing to do with anemia. If anything, he should feel like a million bucks after receiving the transfusion of his own stem cells. It was too soon for the second form of anemia to be attacking his system. He was mentally worn out. He hadn't slept well the night before in the hotel, and he'd been stressed for weeks.

As Blair grabbed some of the bags from the back of the Explorer, she looked up at him. "Let's take a nap first. Explore the area later. Yeah?"

He rounded the SUV and wrapped his arms around her waist. She was still holding the suitcases, so his embrace was awkward, but he kissed her anyway. "I love you."

She smiled. "I love you too."

He grabbed the rest of their stuff and followed her into the cabin. It was small and not nearly as nice as hers, but it didn't matter. As long as the mattress was good, he didn't care about anything else. They didn't plan to stay cooped up inside much. They had discussed hiking and sightseeing, using the cabin as a base—assuming his health remained stable.

After weeks being trapped in the mountains of Colorado, he was looking forward to getting out. Now that he wasn't contagious, he could eat in restaurants and face other people. Anything to fill the time while the clock ticked. He wanted to enjoy every moment with Blair before they had to face the uncertainty of his future.

They dropped their things on the floor and climbed into bed in mutual agreement that sleep was their first priority.

By the following day they were settled in and ready to explore the area. What Dade enjoyed most was that neither of them had been there before, so they were both seeing the beauty for the first time together.

It was cold outside, so there weren't many people around, but true hikers didn't mind about the cold, and Dade didn't care about a damn thing except spending time with Blair. It could have been a hundred degrees or zero, and he still would have enjoyed himself. Luckily, the high was fifty so they could easily wear a coat in the morning and leave it in the car in the afternoon.

Blair was far more carefree than she had been for days, or even weeks. She smiled a lot, both genuinely and at times, forced. He could tell when she put his doom to the back of her mind and when it crept to the front.

At moments when she seemed sullen, he grabbed her, tugged her into his embrace, and kissed the sadness away.

He also noticed she did the same for him. Most of the time he could shake the future out of his head, but there were moments when it invaded his thoughts anyway. A glance at Blair helped.

After hiking for the morning, they found a quaint sandwich shop to have a late lunch. The food was delicious, and Blair had an odd twinkle in her eye. As soon as she finished, she wadded up her sandwich wrap. "There're a couple cute shops along this street. You mind if I go check them out? I won't take long. You could get another coffee while you wait."

He lifted his eyes, his mouth around his next bite.

She was grinning.

He chewed and swallowed and cocked his head to one side. "You? Shopping? Why can't I picture that?" This was not a woman he would have pegged as a shopper. Ever. Not that he cared. In fact, he would gladly go with her and hold her bags if she wanted to explore. But she didn't seem receptive to that idea.

She giggled as she stood. "Everyone shops sometimes. I won't be long." And then she left.

He watched her as she walked out the front door and then passed the picture window. Her blond ponytail was swaying. Her blue eyes had sparkled. She had on jeans that fit her to perfection, and she was wearing her coat over a thick, navy sweater.

Winter was not the time of year to get a good look at a woman's body. Maybe he should encourage her to head for the beach when they left here. Did she own a bikini? He would give anything to lie on the sand and watch her collect seashells.

Would he even be alive or healthy enough to enjoy the view? He vowed that no matter what happened—if he got sick or not—California would be their next destination. Even if he grew weak and it got difficult to move around, he wanted to see Blair in the sunshine, her hair bleached and flying in the wind, her skin tanned. She would be radiant.

He leaned back in his chair and sipped his coffee while he watched people walk by the window. She wasn't gone long. Forty-five minutes at the most. When she reappeared, her hands were empty.

"No luck?" he asked.

"I got a few things. I put them in the SUV already."

"Uh-huh. You planning to show me?"

"Nope."

Interesting. He was smiling as he stood and threw his trash away. Whatever she'd purchased, he was certain he was going to like it. Something about her secrecy was intriguing.

As they left the deli, she tucked her arm inside his and said, "Let's go to dinner tonight. Someplace nice. There are a few restaurants in town."

"Okay. Sounds good. Like a date." He shot her a look. "Damn. We've never been on a date. I've been sleeping with you for weeks, and I haven't ever taken you out. What a shitty boyfriend."

She giggled. "You are a slacker. Make it up to me."

"You're on."

At six o'clock that evening when Blair stepped out of the bedroom ready to go, Dade found out exactly what she had purchased that afternoon. His jaw dropped. He was speechless.

She stood in the doorway, holding the frame. Nervous?

She had no reason to be. Holy God. She wore a black dress that hugged her body to perfection and was obscenely short. In addition, she had on strappy black heels that made her muscular legs look like they belonged on a supermodel.

As his gaze scanned up to her chest, he hesitated, staring at her breasts and the cleavage the low-cut bodice afforded him. Finally, he let his gaze roam to her face. Her hair was down. Curled and tucked behind her ears. She looked like a million bucks. And she was his.

"You gonna say something?" she asked, dropping her hands from the frame and fidgeting her fingers together in front of her.

"Blair?"

That made her roll her eyes.

He headed across the room. When he reached her, he tipped her chin back with one finger and kissed her lips. "You're a gorgeous woman inside and out, even when you're lying around in those tight leggings and loose sweatshirts. But, baby, you look so amazing tonight, I'm probably going to trip over myself."

She smiled. "Glad you like it. I didn't want you to think I can't clean up and be a girl."

"Oh, I'm super clear you're a woman. There was never any doubt of that even the first day I met you in that security uniform and a bun." His gaze wandered down her body and back up. "Maybe we should skip dinner." Sex was sounding so much better.

"Hell, no. We're going out. You owe me a date."

He groaned jokingly as she ducked under his arm and found her coat. She didn't have anything nicer with her than her usual jacket, but he didn't care. It didn't seem to bother her either.

He drove, and when they arrived at the Italian restaurant, he rounded the hood and helped her out of the SUV. "You're going to make me look bad," he said, glancing down at his khaki pants and black dress shirt.

They were the best clothes he had, part of the selection of items Ryan had arranged for him when he first went to the cabin. At the time he'd taken one look and wondered when he would ever have the opportunity to wear anything that nice, including loafers. And now he was eternally grateful.

When they stepped inside, Blair shrugged out of her coat, and Dade hung it up near the door. He set a hand on the small of her back, noticing for the first time that there was an oval cutout in the middle where his hand was now resting on her bare skin.

She shivered when he stroked her back, making him smile.

As the hostess led them to their table, he wondered when she'd ever had the time or energy to learn to walk in heels. She made it look easy, as if she did it every day.

"Do you mind if I have a glass of wine?" she asked him.

"No. Of course not. Go ahead." He didn't think alcohol was a good idea in his precarious state of health, but he would enjoy seeing her unwind a bit and relax.

After they ordered, she sipped her cabernet and watched his face. "I haven't told you how handsome you look."

"Ryan makes an excellent shopper. I'll have to thank him."

"He does. He's a man of many talents. Do you suppose Emily realizes what a catch she has?"

Dade lifted a brow. "You gonna spend the evening gushing over another woman's man while we're eating?" he joked.

She rolled her eyes. "Please. I've known Ryan a long time. He's a good guy, and I love that he found someone to share his life with, but he's not my type."

"What is your type?" He grinned, knowing her response would be entertaining.

She shrugged and took another sip of wine. "I usually go for tall men with broad shoulders and dark eyes. The best ones have been living in a cryostat for ten years so that when I step in front of them, it doesn't matter who I am or what I look like, they're so desperate they fall for me anyway."

Dade laughed. "Glad I could help you out. So, you're saying you've been begging Temple to assign you to a man as soon as he was reanimated so you'd have a chance with him before he had a look at any other woman?"

"Maybe." She giggled. "And then I made sure the other women who came near you were all taken. And then I suggested we run off together to a cabin in the woods and hide. You were never really in any danger. The part about bad guys being after you was all made up." Her eyes were twinkling.

He grabbed her hand from across the table and squeezed her fingers. When he leaned forward, he said the first thing that came to mind, "Please tell me the part about me having some incurable blood disease was also part of your pile of lies to get me alone."

Her face sobered, and she pursed her lips.

"I'm sorry. That was going too far." He gave her hand a squeeze. "I didn't mean to ruin the mood. Tell me what you have on under that dress," he added to shift the conversation back to something light. He released her hand and reached to trail a finger down her neck.

"Guess you'll have to wait and see."

He nearly swallowed his tongue. If she'd bought some sexy lingerie, he might faint when he saw it.

"I can be feminine when the need arises," she stated.

When she shivered under his fingertip, he pulled his hand back. "Like I've told you before, you can't *not* be feminine. Any effort you might have attempted to hide from the world was never successful."

"Thank you." Her face flushed. He liked that look on her. Now he just needed to get through dinner so they could get back to the cabin. He was more intrigued than ever about what was under her dress.

Blair was nervous when they stepped into the cabin after dinner. She had no idea why. It was irrational. She'd been sleeping with Dade for weeks. They'd had sex enough times for her to lose her self-consciousness. But tonight felt different.

For one thing, they had gone on a date. An actual date. One where other humans were around. And she'd enjoyed herself immensely. Dade had been attentive and sexy and funny and handsome. He'd made her blush. He'd made her squirm. He'd given her the perfect evening.

But tonight had undertones to it that couldn't be ignored. There was the looming blood test. Tomorrow they would do a baseline test to see what his numbers were. It would give them something to compare to all future tests. She was stressed about it, and she knew he was too.

She shoved her concerns to the back of her mind when Dade shut the front door and turned toward her. He peeled her coat off and hung it up, and then he held her at arm's length and scanned up and down her body. "You look so damn good in that dress."

"Thank you." She was looking forward to him seeing what was on underneath it, but she also didn't want him to make a big deal out of it. She was a woman. She knew he saw her that way. He always had. Never once from the moment she met him did he ever make her feel less than feminine and sexy. But this was the first time he was going to see her in lace and silk. This was the first time he'd seen her in a dress and heels too. The smoldering look he'd nailed her with all evening spoke volumes.

She shivered when he ran his hands up her bare arms. "You okay?" he asked. "You seem a little distant. You've been quiet for a while."

She shook her head. "I'm fine." *Why the hell am I nervous?*

He stepped closer, gently pulling her into his embrace. His lips landed on her ear. "What's going on, baby? You're not yourself." He ran his hands up her back and threaded them in her hair.

"I'm me," she murmured against his neck in response.

He tipped her head back and nibbled a path to her mouth. His touch calmed her nerves as he reached her mouth and then kissed her. "Your heart is racing," he whispered. "Like we're on a first date and we've never slept together."

"We *are* on a first date. And we were living in a bubble before. It's weird." She was struggling to put her feelings to words, partly because she didn't even know what she was trying to communicate.

One of his hands slid to the small of her back, his warm palm directly on her skin. "How is it weird?"

She licked her lips, trying to answer his question for him and for her. So many thoughts were going through her head. "You were right. I don't own dresses. I don't get fixed up with makeup and hair and heels. I never do that sort of thing."

He nodded slightly. "Are you saying you don't feel comfortable dressed like this? You feel like you're pretending to be someone else?"

"No. It's not that."

He narrowed his gaze, his face so close to hers she could feel his breath on her lips. "Blair, I fell in love with the woman inside you. I don't care about clothes and fancy hair and heels and makeup. Surely, you realize that about me. I love you just the way you are."

"Sure, I think you look amazing tonight, but I didn't mean to make you feel like I prefer this Blair. I don't. It's just a package. Your heart is what I own. Go take the dress off and put on a T-shirt if it makes you more comfortable. I'm sorry if I made you think I liked you better this way. It wasn't my intention."

She shook her head. It was as if she didn't know herself at all. Like she just met the real Blair for the first time. One she had stuffed down and hidden from the world and from herself. "No. It's the opposite."

He gave her a confused frown. "What's the opposite?"

"This is me. I've never felt so sexy in my life. I think I always watched other women and wished I had the guts to be like them, but I didn't. I spent my entire adult life hiding in fatigues, uniforms, buns, and ponytails. I don't know why. Maybe it was safe for some reason. I think I wanted to be seen as tough and hard. I wanted to be equal with the men I worked with. I never wanted them to see me as weak or...female, I guess. I never wanted anyone to fall for me. I didn't want to get hurt. It was easier."

"Baby…"

She had more to say. The thoughts kept coming. "I think I changed when my sister died. I thought she was weak. I never wanted to be weak or out of control. I wanted to be strong, and I wanted everyone around me to know I was badass."

He gave her a half grin. "You *are* badass. But you're also a woman. I have always seen you as both. No matter what you're wearing, I'm always attracted to you." He winced. "Am I butchering this? Making it worse? Maybe I should shut up."

She smiled as she flattened her palm on his chest. "No, you're not butchering anything. I'm the one speaking in circles." She cocked her head to one side. "Let me ask you this. Am I *equally* as attractive to you in leggings and a sports bra as this dress and heels and mystery lingerie?"

He cringed. "This is a trick question."

She giggled. "No. Be honest."

He slowly shook his head. "Well, no… You look fucking hot tonight. Not going to lie. I'm sure I didn't hide my feelings about this dress. But that doesn't mean I think you should wear clothes you aren't comfortable in to please me. I'm a sure thing. I fell hard for you way before I saw you in this dress."

"See, the thing is I kinda liked this new me. I liked dressing up and fixing my hair. And I loved how you looked at me all evening. It made me feel feminine and sexy as hell."

His smile spread. "So, what is the problem here?"

She laughed again. "Yeah, I've made no sense."

He lowered his lips to hers, kissed her senseless, and then trailed a path to her ear again, which got to her every time. "I love you."

She thawed at those words and tipped her head to the side to give him better access to her neck.

When he kissed a path down to her cleavage, her nipples stiffened. She so badly wanted him to look at her with that smoldering intensity when he saw her bra and panty set. She had no idea why it made her nervous. Of course he was going to think she was sexy. He always did.

He backed her up, gradually leading her toward the bedroom. When they arrived, his hand went to the zipper at the back of her neck. He lowered it slowly until the bodice fell loose. When he took a step back, he slid his hands under the dress at her shoulders and let it fall to the floor.

She shivered as his gaze hit her chest and then trailed lower to the tiny black lace thong that matched the barely existent excuse for a bra. All her concerns melted away when he danced his fingers across the upper swell of her chest and murmured, "Jesus."

Her arousal shot through the roof at that one word.

He cupped her heavy breasts and pressed them together, making her cleavage even more pronounced. His thumbs trailed along the edge of lace, dipping under to flick over her nipples.

She rose onto her tiptoes, moaning at the contact. Her heels brought her closer to his chest. She was still significantly shorter than him, but she liked this vantage point better.

His hands trailed down her back to cup her bare cheeks, and then he moaned. "Thong..." When he reached lower to dip his fingers between her legs, a soft noise escaped her lips.

She was wet. So horny. She felt worshipped in this black lace and heels. Feminine. Sexier than she'd ever let herself feel. Because she trusted Dade to treat her with respect while at the same time driving her crazy with his obvious appreciation. He didn't make her feel like an object. He made her feel like a woman. Equal but sexy.

"This is so hot," he whispered as if he read her mind. "I'm so hard."

"Maybe take off some of your clothes too?" She went to work on the buttons on his shirt, her fingers shaking as she slid them each through the holes.

He kissed her everywhere while she worked, making it difficult to concentrate. Chest. Neck. Ear. Cheek. Lips.

When she slid the shirt off his shoulders, he let her go long enough to drop it, and then he went for his pants, unbuttoning them and then lowering the zipper. He kicked off his shoes while he worked and then stepped back to remove the rest of his clothes. The entire time his gaze was on her body.

She felt slightly awkward but only because she wasn't used to this kind of attention. Of course, he had worshipped her before every time they had sex, but she liked the fact that he found her black lace arousing.

When he was finally naked, he grabbed her waist and lifted her onto the bed. He straddled her and lowered his face to her chest, suckling a nipple through the lace.

She arched, pressing her legs together as she grabbed his waist. "Dade..."

He switched to the other breast, the tip abrading against the lace as he flicked his tongue over it. And then he slid down her body, kissing her belly as he went. He nudged her thighs apart with his knee and then settled his torso between her legs, spreading them wide.

She held his shoulders as his lips eased the thin lace edge of the thong. The moment she had put the dainty thing on earlier, she'd gotten horny. Now it was paying off.

His teeth grazed her bare skin as he dipped his face lower, pressed her thighs wider, and finally sucked her clit into his mouth, lace and all. It was so sensual. Naughty. When his tongue dipped under the thin lace to touch her skin directly, she dug her fingers into his shoulders and moaned. She was so close. She'd been tormenting herself all evening in this lingerie, turned on by how he looked at her, and now she was going to come before he took it off.

When she squirmed, he held her hips down and thrust his tongue inside her.

"Oh, God..."

His nose rubbed her clit through the lace, and she came, pulsing waves of need that shook her entire body.

He continued to taste her until she finally relaxed marginally against the mattress. He was smiling as he climbed up her body, nuzzled her breasts, and then kissed her gently on the lips. "Sexiest woman I've ever seen."

She felt a ridiculous grin that seemed to reach her ears as it spread. And then she had a wicked thought. She shoved at his much larger frame, flipping him onto his back next to her. Although realistically he had to "let" her manipulate him like that. She may have been strong, but he was much larger and far stronger than her by now.

He tucked his hands under his head and smiled. His erection bobbed against his belly.

She let her gaze roam up and down his frame, taking in the tight abs, the hard pecs, his tanned smooth skin everywhere. And then she lowered her gaze to his erection and wiggled down his body so that she could lick a line from the base to the tip.

He groaned. "You can't do that if you want me to last."

"Highly overrated," she whispered against his thickness before she sucked him into her mouth. She actually would prefer to suck him off first, and then they could start all over at a more leisurely pace, because she fully intended to have him slide in and out of her for as long as possible during round two.

"Blair…" The sound of her name on his lips heightened her arousal. Reverent. Gravelly.

She sucked him deeper as his hands landed on her head and then threaded in her hair.

"Gonna come," he murmured.

She sucked in her cheeks, adding to the pressure as she took him to the back of her throat.

On a shudder, he came, pulsing ribbons that she swallowed until he was completely spent. Finally, she eased off him. The second he popped free, he pulled her up his body and settled her on his chest. "If sexy thongs and bras are going to cause you to do that often, we should maybe buy fifty sets and stay in the cabin."

She flushed, pushing herself up so that she straddled his chest. Her sex was wet against his pecs, the lace soaked from a combination of her come and his mouth. She reached for the front clasp on her bra, but he stopped her. "Leave it."

Her breasts felt constricted and heavy, swollen from arousal. But the thought of leaving them confined made her hot all over again at the same time. "Okay. But you're going to have to let me lose the thong because I need you inside me as soon as possible."

He shook his head. "Gonna pull it to the side and make love to you with the edge of lace grazing me."

She shuddered, making him smile. And then the breath whooshed from her lungs as she was flipped onto her back again. His mouth was on hers, hot, hungry, desperate. He grabbed her hands and pulled them over her head, the pressure making her arousal rush back to consume her. She bucked her hips against him and wrapped her ankles around his back.

He rested his weight over her, holding her still, further trapping her against the mattress. She loved the dominance. She loved giving herself to him like this. She loved the way he made her feel like she was sexy and desirable and feminine.

She loved that he was stronger than her and she didn't have to be the one in charge of everything. So many sensations bombarded her at once. The way he made love to her mouth and teased her nipples with his chest, and rubbed her sex against his erection.

The kiss lasted forever, and then he shifted her wrists to one hand and reached between their bodies with the other. He tugged her thong to one side and thrust into her so suddenly, she gasped.

Full. Tight. Wet. So good.

When he slid back out and then thrust in again on a grunt, she moaned into his mouth. They were so connected. So together. In sync. In love...

She fought the demon that crept into her mind, not wanting to get overly emotional and ruin this moment. Tears threatened even while they were making love. *Please, God, let me keep this man. Do not take him away from me.*

Never in her life had she been this connected to another human being. So in tune. So happy. She bit back the emotion and focused on the nerve endings currently being stroked over and over, her arousal rising with every slide of him inside her.

Suddenly, she was on the edge, right there. She was so focused on the sensations that she stopped kissing him. Her mouth fell open and her eyes rolled back. And then she was coming, gripping him with the pulse of her channel.

As soon as her body released itself, he was right behind her, his forehead against hers, his mouth millimeters away, a groan vibrating through her.

When he was spent, he remained buried inside her, panting, smiling. He looked so peaceful and happy. She wanted to capture that look and remember it for the rest of her life. For several long seconds he forgot his problems and pure joy surrounded him.

He sighed as he blinked his eyes open to look down at her. "Was I too rough?"

She furrowed her brow. "What? Of course not. That was perfect. Amazing. I loved it."

He slid out of her and eased onto his side next to her, one leg still trapping her to the bed, his hand releasing hers to cup her face. His next words were breathy and unexpected. "I'm taking you back to that store to by ten sets of lingerie tomorrow."

She giggled. "You think that's practical? I mean, it's not the sort of thing women wear hiking or working out. I'm still badass on the outside. Most of the time."

He kissed her reverently, staring down at her. "Baby, you have no idea what other women wear under their hiking clothes. Maybe you aren't the only one who likes lace and silk. If it makes you feel sexy, you should wear it. I'll spend my days wondering what you have on under your jeans while I follow you around like a puppy."

"Mmm. I might like that plan. If I keep that look of awe and wonder in your eyes, it will be worth it."

"See? What time does the store open?"

CHAPTER 20

Three weeks later…

The sun was just peeking in the window of the cottage when Blair opened her eyes to find Dade propped on an elbow, staring down at her. The sound of the ocean waves combined with the smell of salt in the air usually soothed her, but not this morning.

They had left the window that faced the beach open from the moment they'd arrived a week ago. Neither of them cared about the humidity or the salt. They simply enjoyed the feel of fresh air and sounds of nature after weeks of being cooped up and cold all the time.

Dade brushed a lock of hair from her face and then danced his fingers down to trace the edge of the negligee she wore. His expression was serious. "I love you so much it hurts."

She swallowed back emotion and reached for his hand, covering it with her own. "I love you too." She held his gaze for a while. "We don't have to do this, you know. There are no rules. We can wait another week or two or a month or forever."

He shook his head. "Nope. We agreed on today. It's time to find out once and for all."

They had drawn his blood for the first time three weeks ago, the baseline. However, the following week, when they ran the test, they didn't look at the results. By mutual agreement, they decided to ignore the results for three weeks.

Some days she would sit for hours staring at the waves, worrying about what they would find. She kept reminding herself that Dade didn't have any discernible symptoms to indicate the transplant didn't work. It was impossible to know how long it would take for him to start feeling poorly however. There simply wasn't anyone to compare it to.

Even though he had started to feel lethargic and had gotten several headaches before he received the cure for AP12, he claimed he had felt fine since they left her cabin. They were under so much stress, she wouldn't be surprised if he felt tired anyway. It wouldn't necessarily mean anything.

It was possible the experimental autologous stem cell transplant was buying him time, slowing down the process. However, even if that were the case, they would be seeing a drop in both white and red blood cells with each test. At least a subtle drop.

She watched his face closely, knowing how huge this was. For both of them. "You want to go for a walk on the beach first? Maybe grab some breakfast at that little coffee shop?" Was she stalling for his benefit or hers?

He shook his head. "Let's just do it."

"Okay." She wormed her arm around him and pulled him down for a kiss, holding him tight. "No matter what, I love you."

"I know." He buried his face in her hair. When he pulled back, he cleared his throat. "I need to tell you something."

She frowned.

"When I signed those papers for the executor that day, there were two documents."

She nodded, vaguely remembering that fact.

"One was to claim my inheritance. The other was my own will. It leaves everything to you in the event something happens to me."

She gasped. "Dade... Are you serious?"

"Of course."

A tear fell from her eye. She choked up with emotion.

"Baby, don't cry." He wiped the tear with his thumb and cupped her face. One side of his mouth lifted in that half grin before he added, "Who else was I going to leave the money to? I mean, I don't have other friends."

She rolled her eyes. "Don't try to make light of this."

He kissed her nose and then sobered. "I want you to be able to do whatever you want with your life. You've left your job and your friends for me. You've been isolated for two months because of me. I know you're running out of time. Soon you'll need to let Temple know if you're returning or resigning.

"No matter what happens, I want you to have options. You can go back to your job if you want, or you can start a new career, or if you're frugal enough you can live off the money for a very long time."

"Stop talking like I'll be making that decision alone. I won't be."

He blew out a breath. "Yeah, well, I wanted you to know. No matter what the outcome, I'll support your choices."

She smirked. "You think I've been pining away for my job, waiting for the opportunity to let you know I intended to go back to the bunker next month and take up where I left off?"

"No. I'm just telling you that you have options."

"I don't have options, you big dork." She lifted her head and kissed his nose. When she let her head fall back to the pillow, she licked her lips and faced him again. "There's something I need to tell you too."

His eyes widened and he held her waist tighter.

She didn't make him wait. "Ryan gave me an envelope with

instructions when we left the cabin that day. I think he meant for those instructions to begin today."

"What did it say?"

"I don't know. I didn't open it yet. I couldn't do it without you, and there was no way I could keep a secret from you either."

He grinned. "You kept the existence of the envelope a secret."

"Well, there's that. But I mean the contents. I have no idea what he said."

"Let's open it after."

She nodded agreement, and then she rolled away from him. "Let's do this so you'll stop being all melancholy."

He rolled the other direction and headed for the bathroom. When he came out, she was at the table in their cottage with the ominous case open. She pointed at the chair as if she were playing nurse.

He shook his head as he approached. "I can't take you seriously when you're wearing those flimsy nighties." He pulled her in close and ran his hand up her back over the silky pink material. The fact that it was pink was the icing on the cake.

His badass bodyguard had a deep feminine streak that made his body jump to attention every time he saw her wearing another one of her purchases. And it happened often because it turned out she loved the look he nailed her with when she wore them, and they often spent hours in the cottage wearing very little clothing.

She lifted the syringe and held it out. "You want me to do it?"

He could do it himself, but he'd taught her how the second week. Somehow, it was weird drawing his own blood. "Yes." He sat on the chair she'd pulled out and prayed to God he would be spending the rest of the day celebrating with his mouth all over that negligée.

He tried not to get his hopes up, but it was hard. Half the time when he watched her moving around their space or lounging on the beach or reading or attempting to cook or sleeping or making love, he couldn't imagine that God would take this away from him. The other half the time he was scared out of his mind with worry about what would happen to her if he left her.

She didn't say a word as she carefully drew his blood and then handed him the syringe.

He took the vial from her and set up the test station, putting several drops of blood on the scanner and then closing the lid. They would need to wait two minutes for the results. The machine kept a log of each scan. All they had to do was look back at the reports and compare them.

He turned around in the chair and pulled her between his legs. He was only wearing boxer shorts, so when he pressed his head to her chest and wrapped his arms around her waist, his skin flattened against the cool, silk material of her nightie.

He clutched her like that, tighter than necessary, probably almost hurting her. He kept his emotions in check also. He held his breath most of that long two minutes too. Neither of them spoke. Blair stroked his hair and his neck and his shoulders.

When the timer pinged to let them know the test results were completed, he took a deep breath and lifted his gaze to hers. "Ready?"

She shook her head. "I'll never be ready, but I'm strong."

He smiled. "That you are." Was she strong enough for seriously bad news, though?

He released her, turned slowly, and hit the button on the side of the machine that would spit out a printout of the cumulative results.

Blair's hands were on his shoulders, her grip firm.

He waited for the paper to stop coming out, tore it off, and then flattened it in front of him. After a long, slow inhale, he held his breath again as his eyes scanned the information.

He glanced at the baseline results and took in the numbers. His gaze shifted quickly to the next week and then the next and finally the last. And then he exhaled that breath with a whoosh and went back to the first result again to make sure he'd read each line correctly.

"Dade?"

He set his finger on the first result, picking the white blood cell count.

She leaned forward.

When he was confident she had seen that first number, he tapped the second.

"That's good, right? You want the number to be higher, right?"

He tapped the third and then the forth. And then he spun around, grabbed her waist, and smiled. "It's excellent. It's working."

Tears ran down her face, but she was not alone. He couldn't keep from crying right alongside her. In fact, he let out a primal cry of happiness, jumped to his feet, and lifted her by the waist. She wrapped her legs around him as he spun around and flung them both onto the bed.

With her underneath him, her ankles locked at his lower back, her cheeks covered with tears, he cupped her face and smiled. "It's working," he repeated. "I almost don't believe it."

She held his face in her smaller hands too. "I'm so damn happy I can't catch my breath."

He nuzzled her neck and kissed a path to her lips. "Thank you. Thank you for sticking with me. Thank you for holding me through this. I couldn't have done it without you."

She smiled, still crying. "I wouldn't have been anyplace else."

He drew in a deep breath. "We should call Ryan." They had not yet made contact with Ryan since they left her cabin. They had a throwaway phone for this purpose, but so far they hadn't needed it. They had no reason to call until they knew something. Though they realized Ryan was probably out of his mind with worry since they'd taken so long to report.

She wiped the tears from her face. "Yes."

Dade pushed off her, rushed across the room, and rummaged through their belongings for the phone. It would be an hour later there, but still early.

The phone rang three times before Ryan finally answered. "Hello?" His voice was low, a whisper. He had probably been in bed with Emily and rushed to find someplace private to answer.

"It worked," Dade announced, unable to contain his excitement as he hauled Blair against his chest again. "It fucking worked."

Ryan let out a long exhale. "Fuck me. I'm so damn glad." His voice was so low, Dade could barely hear it.

"I know you can't talk. I'll send a vial of blood to you at the P.O. box you gave us. But I feel very confident."

"Thank God. Listen, I need to speak to you before you talk to anyone else. Can you call me back in five minutes?"

"Yes. Of course."

The line went dead, and Dade lowered the phone.

"What do you think he wants?"

"Probably just needed to find someplace more private."

"You think he would keep this from Emily?"

Dade shrugged. "I don't know."

Blair still sat on the edge of the bed. Dade continued to hold her against him, unwilling to stop touching her, possibly forever.

When the five minutes had passed, he sat next to her and held the phone between them, putting the call on speaker.

"Sorry about that," Ryan greeted them with. "Listen, I don't have much time. Did you read my letter?"

"Not yet," Dade said. "We were going to do that next."

"Good. Read it. Think about it. Call me in a few days and tell me what you think."

Dade glanced at Blair, his brows furrowed. Strange conversation.

"I assume you have a proposition?" It would have to be

something he'd thought about and planned more than a month ago.

"Yes. Like I said, take a few days. Discuss it. In the meantime, don't tell anyone about your results. Not a soul. Stay hidden. Lay low."

Dade glanced at Blair, frowning. He hadn't thought much about what he would do after reading the results, but it hadn't occurred to him he was in so much danger that he would need to remain hidden forever. "You think it's that dangerous?"

"Yes. I don't know who to trust. I can't sleep at night worrying about who might be leaking information about everyone and why."

"You have eleven reanimated people in the bunker now, right?"

"Yes. And I think this is the safest place for everyone for the time being. I don't like the thought of anyone leaving here. Moving you out was sticky. Made me nervous. Luckily, no one found you. Now, you're safe. As safe as you can be."

Dade glanced at Blair whose face was pale. He spoke into the phone again while he watched her. "Did someone attempt to find me?"

"Yes. I have no idea who, but someone broke into that hotel and tore it apart. I bet they were pretty pissed when they realized they'd been played."

"Fuck." The one word came out as a hiss while Blair winced. She was biting her lower lip. "Okay," he said into the phone. "Give us a few days. I'm going to destroy this phone. I'll call you on another."

"Perfect. Overnight me the sample. I'll confirm the results. Call me in three days at ten o'clock in the morning on this burner phone still. I'll keep it as long as I can. I'll make sure I'm outside getting some air. If I don't answer, you'll know I couldn't. Try again later."

"Got it. Please be careful." If anyone found out Ryan had removed that tracker and was digging around trying to figure out who was stalking the members of Dade's team, his life could be in danger too.

The call went dead.

"Jesus," Blair murmured. "There was a desperation in his voice I've never heard before. Ryan is an intense guy, but not like that."

Dade nodded. "I heard it too."

"What are you thinking?" she asked, threading her fingers with his.

He stared at her, wondering how she would respond to the crazy ideas running through his head.

Suddenly, she smiled. "We're going rogue, aren't we? We're going to figure this thing out. Pretend you died and find that fucking mole."

Damn, he loved her. He really loved her. "I'd bet my life that's what's in the letter. Where is it?"

She shoved off the bed, padded to her suitcase, and pulled it from a side pocket. When she returned, he tore it open, and they both leaned over to read the short note that confirmed their suspicion. Ryan needed their help.

"You ready for a bit of adventure?" he asked. Dade hadn't known Ryan long, but he'd spent enough time with Tushar and Trish's son to know how frustrated the man was about the leaks. It wasn't surprising he would ask the two of them to help from the outside. Ryan would think it was a huge thing to ask. Dade didn't need three seconds to agree to the plan, and he knew Blair wouldn't either. Three days was overkill.

Blair's face lit up. "Hell, yes." She jumped to her feet and climbed onto his lap, straddling him. "I mean, I might have a few other things I want to do before we hit the road, but yes. Let's solve this mystery."

He cupped her ass, drawing her warmth closer to his erection. "You have a few things you'd like to do first?" he teased.

"Definitely." She kissed him soundly and then spoke again. "I just found my new calling."

"Private detective?"

"Yep. Now I just need to find a way to tell Temple I'm too distraught to return to work and that I'm planning to go off somewhere and lick my wounds for a long time."

"Maybe a letter would be sufficient. We could mail it from some random post office as we're passing through somewhere. Totally untraceable."

"Perfect."

He closed his eyes, drawing her face closer. "You don't have to do this, you know. We didn't even fully discuss it."

"Are you kidding? I feel like I just won the lottery. The least I can do is take off with my man and do everything in my power to ensure all twenty-one other people inside that bunker can enjoy long happy lives. They can't be expected to stay at that facility forever."

He nibbled a path to her chest. "Enough plotting. Badass Blair can wait until I'm finished ravaging soft, sexy Blair before she gets carried away."

She giggled. Damn, he loved that sound. And then she shoved him backward. "I don't know. I have a lot of pent-up energy. I might need to channel that into dominant, topping, badass-in-bed Blair this time around."

He grinned. "Be my guest. Turns out I love both of those women." His heart was full as her hands landed on his chest and trailed down toward heaven.

CHAPTER 21

Three days later...

Zeke was leaning over a microscope, examining the specimen for a rare disease the team was working on when Temple came into the lab. The only other person in the room was Ryan who had been quietly working behind him for hours.

"Ah, Ryan, glad I caught you. Emily said you had lab results for Dade."

This was news to Zeke. He swiveled his stool around to find Ryan leaning back in his chair rubbing his forehead. He looked exhausted and frustrated. He nodded toward the specimen in front of him. "Yeah." He shook his head.

Temple cringed. "The treatment didn't work?" Her face paled, and her shoulders slumped.

Zeke stiffened. He thought he was going to vomit. Dade was a good friend of his. Why hadn't Ryan said anything? A flood of emotions filled him. Sadness. Grief. Anger. He didn't move.

Ryan swallowed. "It was a longshot."

"How long does he have? Is there anything we can do?" Temple asked.

Ryan shook his head. "It's hard to say. Maybe a month. Could be more. Could be less. It's impossible to know since we don't have any other cases to compare it to. We've exhausted our options."

"Does he want to come back to the bunker? What about Blair?" Temple gripped the doorframe with both hands.

Ryan shook his head. "No. He doesn't want anyone to fuss over him. He wants to spend the rest of his time in peace. Blair is staying with him. She's sending you her resignation."

"Of course." She wiped a tear from her eye. "Dammit." After a deep breath, she said, "Please tell him he's in our thoughts. If there's anything we can do…"

"I will."

Temple sighed as she walked away.

Zeke stood, needing to see for himself. He was a scientist. He wanted proof. It was in his veins. His body felt heavy as he stepped up beside Ryan and leaned over the microscope to look at the blood sample.

For a moment, he thought his vision must be deceiving him. He blinked several times and took another look. When he lifted his face, confused as hell, Ryan was staring at him with his lips pursed, shaking his head subtly.

For a second, Zeke didn't know what the fuck was going on. He needed more information. "I think I'll take a walk and clear my head."

Ryan pushed from his chair. "I'll go with you. Fresh air will do us some good. Just let me clean this mess up." Ryan destroyed the sample and put it in the biohazard container and then turned off the equipment.

Zeke was shaking as he walked out the front door of the bunker, Ryan on his heels. He strolled away from the bunker silently, hands in his pockets. When they were a safe distance away, he stopped and toed the dirt at his feet. "What the fuck is going on?" he whispered. He knew instinctively Ryan had lied for a reason.

"There's a mole, Zeke."

"I get that, but it isn't Temple."

"I agree, but I don't trust anyone. Somehow every damn thing that happens in this bunker gets leaked. Maybe it's one of Temple's superiors. Obviously, she answers to someone. I have no doubt in my mind that right this second she's reporting to someone higher up to let them know that Dade isn't going to make it."

Zeke nodded. "You're right."

"I hate lying to her. This is the first time I have, but Dade deserves a chance at life, and the only way for him to have that is if everyone thinks he's dead."

Zeke lifted his gaze. "Blair's going to stay with him?"

"Yes. She'll tender her resignation, saying that she's too distraught to return. Dade's grandfather left him plenty of money to live off of for a long time."

"Who knows about this?"

"You. And me."

"Jesus." Zeke walked away a few steps and came back. "Why did you tell me? You could have left me out of it."

"For a few reasons. One, you're Dade's best friend. I know you would never do anything to jeopardize his life. Two, you're obviously not the mole. You weren't even reanimated when this all started. Three, I'm gonna need your help."

"My help? With what?"

"Finding the mole. I don't want anyone else on your team to get kidnapped, shot at, or killed."

Zeke fisted his hands in his pockets. He thought about Ryan's request for a while, taking deep breaths. "Of course. I'm in."

"There's one more thing," Ryan said, his face serious.

"What?"

"Dade and Blair are going to help us."

Zeke flinched, his spine going rigid. "Seriously?"

"Yes. We're going to feed them any information we get using a burner phone and they're going to work from the outside to help us. We're going to look into every leak, start from the bottom up, find out who had access to what information, and begin eliminating possibilities. If the leak is coming from higher up, then we'll remove every rung on the ladder until we get to the top. It's not just our people being compromised, it's the entirety of Project DEEP. And it's every person in the world who is counting on our research to cure infectious diseases."

Zeke slowly smiled. "I love this plan."

AUTHOR'S NOTE

I hope you enjoyed book three in the *Project DEEP* series. Please enjoy the following excerpt for book four in the series, *Reviving Zeke.*

REVIVING ZEKE

PROJECT DEEP (BOOK FOUR)

"Put me to work. I don't care if you want me to take out the trash, vacuum the floors, clean toilets, or find a cure for Ebola, but I'll lose my mind soon if you don't give me a task."

Michelle lifted her gaze from the paperwork she was going over with her boss, General Temple Levenson, in the general's office. Standing in the doorway, scowling, was one of the latest patients to be reanimated by the Project DEEP team—Zeke Holleran.

Of the eight people who had been revived so far, Zeke was Michelle's least favorite. He seemed permanently angry. Sure, he was ridiculously good looking, but his brow was always furrowed, and he rarely spoke to anyone.

Temple leaned back in her chair. "You've been awake only three weeks. You should be concentrating on standing, walking, using a fork."

He narrowed his gaze. "I think I've got those things down, Temple. I realize you haven't seen me for ten years, but do you remember me sitting around with my feet up?"

She chuckled. "No. Definitely not." Temple was the link between every member of both teams—the old and the new. She had been there from the beginning, so Zeke knew her as well or better than anyone who had been hired in the bunker in the last few years.

"Look, I realize you have no system in place to pay any of us yet, but you're going to have a mutiny on your hands soon if you don't figure out something for us to do. We're scientists. We may be behind on the latest developments, but we each need to figure out if we're willing to put in the work or change professions. The only way that's going to happen is if you give out some assignments."

Michelle could see his point. If she were in his shoes, she would be crawling out of her skin.

"Do you still feel solid as an immunologist? Any memory problems?" Temple glanced from Zeke to Michelle.

Oh no. Hell, no. Please, God, no.

"I'm solid." Zeke lifted a brow.

"And you're sure you want to continue with Project DEEP? You realize you have options. No one is required to stay. We can relocate you. Provide you with a new identity so you can start over."

"Not a chance. This is my life."

Temple nodded slowly. "Well, it's only been three weeks. You don't have to decide anything today, but if you want to get back to work, why don't you shadow Michelle? She's also an immunologist. She can bring you up to speed."

Zeke shifted his gaze toward Michelle, seeming to just that moment notice she was in the room. He was still frowning, but she refused to take it personally. He knew nothing about her, and he scowled like that at everyone.

That didn't mean she wanted to work with him. Shit.

Zeke hesitated. Was he scrutinizing her?

She stood straighter to her full height of five nine and crossed her arms as if this were a standoff. "Join me any time you'd like. I know you're still gaining strength. I'll understand if you want to start slow. Maybe a few hours a day?" She knew she sounded snarky, and she fully intended to. Jesus, the man could melt iron with his looks.

"I'm not having trouble staying awake, for God's sake. I'm just not quite up to a marathon."

"Well, everything around here is a marathon. That's why I'm suggesting you not attempt to enter the competition. Ease in. See what you remember and where the holes are. Then we can take it from there."

"Excellent," Temple interrupted. "Now, I've got a meeting in the conference room. I trust you two can continue this tête-à-tête elsewhere?" She glanced at Michelle as she stood, eyebrows lifted. She gave her a more pointed glare as she shuffled toward the door.

Great. Now Temple didn't think Michelle could play nice. Then again, Michelle wasn't at all sure she was capable herself.

She followed Temple out of the office as Zeke backed into the hallway also. Temple walked away, and Michelle pasted on a smile. "You want to start tomorrow?"

"Now's fine. Show me what you're working on." He swept a hand in the direction of the wing of the bunker where most of the medical personnel worked. At least he was a gentleman.

He followed her while she tried to imagine how she was going to live through this ordeal. She was backed up with projects that needed attention. Meanwhile, the bunker was quickly filling with newly reanimated staff whose skills were ten years behind. Next week, there would be four more joining the group.

The bunker was getting crowded, and tensions were high because no one was supposed to leave the bunker without permission.

The only way anyone could leave the bunker was if they chose to take a new name and relocate to start a new life. So far, no one had opted to leave. As more of them awoke, Michelle had little doubt some of them would quickly decide they didn't want any part of this chaos.

When Michelle rounded the doorway leading to the main lab, she found several coworkers already buried in work.

"For some reason, the lab looks smaller than it did the last time I was here," Zeke murmured.

"Well, I wasn't here ten years ago, but Tushar, Trish, and Emily have all confirmed there have been few changes to anything. With the exception of the additional attached housing units, this section of the bunker hasn't undergone much of an overhaul."

"Oh, trust me. I would remember. I was just here a month ago in my mind."

"Right." She nodded as she led him to a workstation. She was aware of how each of the reanimated scientists perceived the passage of time, but it was still eerie. As far as the original team was concerned, they'd been in a sort of coma with no awareness that a decade had gone by.

Zeke picked up a notebook she'd been using before she went to see Temple. "How can you even read this?" he asked, scowling.

She inhaled slowly, forcing herself not to slap him. If he said one more condescending thing, she wasn't sure she could hold back. "I don't need to. Everything important is in the computer. I just keep a notebook next to me to jot something down quickly if I need to."

"The computer..." He glanced at the laptop open on the desk area.

The room was bustling with six other people working and talking over each other. Sometimes Michelle felt like she worked for a major newspaper always on the cusp of an important story instead of in a government bunker.

Project DEEP was the thankfully short abbreviation for Disease & Epidemic Eradication & Prevention. Not a soul used that term. Half of them couldn't even remember it.

"Yeah, I've also come to realize your team didn't rely as heavily on computers ten years ago."

"We used computers, of course, but I've never trusted them enough to rely on them not eating my data or losing it somehow in the ether," he grumbled.

"They've improved a lot in the last decade. We back up everything multiple times into a cloud and onto external hard drives. It's all safe."

He lifted a brow. "I'm clear on how the computer works. We backed up everything even in the dark ages a decade ago, but if I can't hold it in my hands, it doesn't feel safe."

Was he going to argue with her like this constantly? She was losing her patience, and they hadn't even started yet. Great. This was going to be so much fun. "You might like to take a refresher course on computers to get up to speed. Kate, Grayson, and Colton were going to sit down with our tech guy and brush up." The three people she was referring to had been reanimated at the same time as Zeke. They were coworkers of Zeke's.

Zeke ignored her offer. Perhaps he didn't play nice with others even a decade ago. "I'll just stick to paper for now."

"Okay. Suit yourself."

"What's most urgent?" he asked, taking a seat in the rolling chair as he lifted the printout of a spreadsheet to scrutinize. He didn't look her in the eye. It was annoying as hell and somewhat rude or condescending. She wasn't sure which.

If this guy even so much as insinuated that she wasn't as good as him because she was a woman, she truly would kill him with her bare hands. She wasn't sure why she got that particular vibe, but it stuck. "Myasthenia Gravis," she said.

He nodded slowly, peering into the microscope in front of him and then glancing around at the samples on the desk. "It makes me kind of sick to my stomach to realize how little advancement has been made in the last ten years in some areas of research," he told the microscope.

She chose to pretend he wasn't criticizing her in particular or even the Project DEEP team. *He's just making an observation. Don't take it personally.*

"Why is this disease at the forefront right now?" he asked the desk.

She wanted to grab his chin and force him to make eye contact with her. Instead, she took a deep breath and answered his question. They were going to be working closely. She needed to find a way to stifle this animosity. "There has been an unusual surge in occurrences in the last few years. No one knows the causes, and we're still no closer to a cure."

"I see."

"I'll give you some time to look over the data." she stated, hoping to get away from him so she could breathe again. It was too bad he was so foul. If his brow weren't knitted together and he actually smiled and relaxed his shoulders, women would do a double-take when they walked by.

At a glance, he was attractive. Six feet tall. Green eyes she'd only glimpsed. Broad shoulders. Brown wavy hair. He could even be sexy. But instead, he was a bit of an ass.

"Let me know if you need anything. Or ask anyone in the room. We're all friendly." *Except you.*

Keeping his head tipped down, he lifted his gaze alone to meet hers. It was the first time he made eye contact with her. "I have a PhD in immunology from Harvard. I think I'll be fine."

"Good for you," she returned. "I have a matching PhD from Emory that is ten years newer than yours." Without another word, she turned around and left the room, praying she could make it to someplace private before she stomped her feet in frustration.

ALSO BY BECCA JAMESON

Seattle Doms:

Salacious Exposure by Becca Jameson

Salacious Desires By Kate Oliver

Salacious Attraction by Becca Jameson

Salacious Indulgence by Kate Oliver

Salacious Devotion by Becca Jameson

Salacious Surrender by Kate Oliver

Danger Bluff:

Rocco

Hawking

Kestrel

Magnus

Phoenix

Caesar

Roses and Thorns:

Marigold

Oleander

Jasmine

Tulip

Daffodil

Lily

Roses and Thorns Box Set One

Roses and Thorns Box Set Two

Hideout

Haven

The Wanderers Box Set One

The Wanderers Box Set Two

Surrender:

Raising Lucy

Teaching Abby

Leaving Roman

Choosing Kellen

Pleasing Josie

Honoring Hudson

Nurturing Britney

Charming Colton

Convincing Leah

Rewarding Avery

Impressing Brett

Guiding Cassandra

Chasing Amber

Controlling Natasha

Provoking Camden

Surrender Box Set One

Surrender Box Set Two

Surrender Box Set Three

Surrender Box Set Four

Open Skies:

Layover

Redeye

Project DEEP:

Reviving Emily

Reviving Trish

Reviving Dade

Reviving Zeke

Reviving Graham

Reviving Bianca

Reviving Olivia

Project DEEP Box Set One

Project DEEP Box Set Two

SEALs in Paradise:

Hot SEAL, Red Wine

Hot SEAL, Australian Nights

Hot SEAL, Cold Feet

Hot SEAL, April's Fool

Hot SEAL, Brown-Eyed Girl

Dark Falls:

Dark Nightmares

Club Zodiac:

Training Sasha

Obeying Rowen

Collaring Brooke

Mastering Rayne

Trusting Aaron

Claiming London

Sharing Charlotte

Taming Rex

Tempting Elizabeth

Club Zodiac Box Set One

Club Zodiac Box Set Two

Club Zodiac Box Set Three

The Art of Kink:

Pose

Paint

Sculpt

Arcadian Bears:

Grizzly Mountain

Grizzly Beginning

Grizzly Secret

Grizzly Promise

Grizzly Survival

Grizzly Perfection

Arcadian Bears Box Set One

Arcadian Bears Box Set Two

Sleeper SEALs:

Saving Zola

Spring Training:

Catching Zia

Catching Lily

Catching Ava

Spring Training Box Set

The Underground series:

Force

Clinch

Guard

Submit

Thrust

Torque

The Underground Box Set One

The Underground Box Set Two

Wolf Masters series:

Kara's Wolves

Lindsey's Wolves

Jessica's Wolves

Alyssa's Wolves

Tessa's Wolf

Rebecca's Wolves

Melinda's Wolves

Laurie's Wolves

Amanda's Wolves

Sharon's Wolves

Wolf Masters Box Set One

Wolf Masters Box Set Two

Claiming Her series:

The Rules

The Game

The Prize

Claiming Her Box Set

Emergence series:

Bound to be Taken

Bound to be Tamed

Bound to be Tested

Bound to be Tempted

Emergence Box Set

The Fight Club series:

Come

Perv

Need

Hers

Want

Lust

The Fight Club Box Set One

The Fight Club Box Set Two

Wolf Gatherings series:

Tarnished

Dominated

Completed

Redeemed

Abandoned

Betrayed

Wolf Gatherings Box Set One

Wolf Gathering Box Set Two

Durham Wolves series:

Rescue in the Smokies

Fire in the Smokies

Freedom in the Smokies

Durham Wolves Box Set

Stand Alone Books:

Blind with Love

Guarding the Truth

Out of the Smoke

Abducting His Mate

Wolf Trinity

Frostbitten

A Princess for Cale/A Princess for Cain

Severed Dreams

Where Alphas Dominate

ABOUT THE AUTHOR

Becca Jameson is a USA Today best-selling author of over 150 books. She is well-known for her Wolf Masters series, her Fight Club series, and her Surrender series. She currently lives in Houston, Texas, with her husband. Two grown kids pop in every once in a while, too! She is loving this journey and has dabbled in a variety of genres, including paranormal, sports romance, military, reverse harem, dark romance, suspense, dystopian, BDSM, and Daddy Dom.

A total night owl, Becca writes late at night, sequestering herself in her office with a glass of red wine and a bar of dark chocolate, her fingers flying across the keyboard as her characters weave their own stories.

During the day--which never starts before ten in the morning!-- she can be found walking, running errands, or reading in her favorite hammock chair!

...where Alphas dominate...

Becca's Newsletter Sign-up

Join my Facebook fan group, Becca's Bibliomaniacs, for the most up-to-date information, random excerpts while I work, giveaways, and fun release parties!

Facebook Fan Group:
Becca's Bibliomaniacs

Contact Becca:
www.beccajameson.com
beccajameson4@aol.com

facebook.com/becca.jameson.18
x.com/beccajameson
instagram.com/becca.jameson
bookbub.com/authors/becca-jameson
goodreads.com/beccajameson
amazon.com/author/beccajameson

www.ingramcontent.com/pod-product-compliance
Lightning Source LLC
Chambersburg PA
CBHW071327250626
47159CB00004B/1499